A DEATH IN TWO PARTS

A DEATH IN
TWO PARTS

Jane Aiken Hodge

This first world edition published in Great Britain 2000 by
SEVERN HOUSE PUBLISHERS LTD of
9–15 High Street, Sutton, Surrey SM1 1DF.
This first world edition published in the U.S.A. 2000 by
SEVERN HOUSE PUBLISHERS INC of
595 Madison Avenue, New York, N.Y. 10022.

British Library Cataloguing in Publication Data

Hodge,   Jane Aiken,   1917-
    A death in two parts
    1.Detective and mystery stories
    I. Title
    823.9'14 [F]

    ISBN 0-7278-5532-8

Typeset by Palimpsest Book Production Ltd.
Polmont, Stirlingshire, Scotland.
Printed and bound in Great Britain by
MPG Books Ltd, Bodmin, Cornwall.

To the Reader

I wrote the first half of this book in 1950, when we were living in Essex, and was amused to find, when I happened on it a while ago, that I had set it in Lewes, where I live now. I am not sure whether I stopped half-way through because I was busy with my first daughter, or because I had painted myself into a plot corner and could not get out. At any rate, it seemed a challenge, and I have enjoyed solving the problem I set myself. The geography of Lewes was a bit erratic (I had only been there once), so for that and other reasons I have invented Leyning, which must lie somewhere Ditchling way. The house on Leyning High Street is an amalgam of mine and a friend's, but the people are entirely my own.

Part One

1950

One

P atience Smith put her glass down slowly. "You mean," she said, "that there's no money at all?"

Her companion looked around the crowded restaurant – anywhere but at her. "I'm very much afraid that's it," Paul Protheroe said. "I can't tell you how sorry I am – anything I can do, of course . . . I shall be only too delighted." It did not ring altogether true, and, perhaps aware of this, he summoned their waiter and made amends by ordering her an elaborate lunch.

She was still taking in the news he had given her. "The allowance I've had has exhausted the fund?"

"I'm afraid that's it. The payments were made automatically, you see, under your father's will and it was only when we came to take stock on your twenty-first birthday that we discovered. As a matter of fact – " he hesitated – "the last allowance cheque was by way of being an advance . . . but of course we'll forget about that. Ah, this looks good." He watched the waiter's ministrations, gravely approving.

For the moment Patience ignored hors d'œuvres. "You mean," she said, "I'm not just penniless, I'm in debt."

"Oh come; it's not really so bad as that. We're not going

to dun you. After all, I am by way of being your cousin as well as your lawyer."

"Yes." She was not particularly enthusiastic about it. "Wasn't it rather odd of Father?"

"Oh, no. He couldn't have had any idea this would happen. You see, his death and your mother's came so close together – the death duties were pretty steep . . . and then how was he to know how this government was going to play about with the value of money?" It was a subject on which she had heard him many times before, and she took the next few sentences for granted, occupying herself, meanwhile, with a vision of her father, prosperous, financial and withdrawn, in his study. "And of course," her cousin was winding up, "he hadn't allowed for the length of your minority."

"No," she said, "he would hardly have expected that."

"Of course not. I am sure he and my father thought they were making the best possible decision when they tied that fund of yours up so tight, all those years ago, when you were born."

"I'm only twenty-one," she intervened. "Don't make me sound too ancient, please!"

"I beg your pardon." He did not much like being interrupted. "But as I was trying to say, I myself have always felt, since I took over your fund, that it was unfortunate that they had never thought to reconsider it. If we could have had the handling of your money it would have been a very different story today." He paused. "Well, no use crying over spilt milk, and I'd be the last to say anything against your father."

"I should think not. He paid for your education, didn't he?

4

After *your* father died in that accident?" Paul Protheroe was only a few years older than she was, which had always made his superior assumptions harder to bear.

"He did indeed, and that's why I want to do everything I can to help you now." He looked slightly taken aback, as if he had not expected the statement to come out quite so positively.

"It's good of you. Yes, thank you, I've finished." She let the waiter take away her almost untouched hors d'œuvres.

Paul summoned the wine waiter with a flourish and ordered burgundy. "You mustn't let it get you down, you know."

She tackled seasonable turkey with a will. Anything rather than his sympathy. "No, of course not. I was just thinking . . ."

"Well?"

"No, it's no use. I was wondering if I could borrow from college to finish the year – it seems silly to be so near one's degree and not get it, but two terms would be a lot of money."

"Yes, I suppose they would. It's hard to know what to advise. As you know, I've never cared much about all this higher education for women myself – a waste of time, if you ask me."

"I know." They had had this conversation many times before. "One of these days the right man will come along and I'll forget the whole box of tricks!"

"Exactly." If he knew she was mocking him, he ignored it. "I suppose he hasn't by any chance?"

"No." If she said it a little too firmly, he showed no sign of noticing. "That's your solution, is it?"

5

"Well, it would take care of you, of course. But if there's no one . . . What were you thinking of doing?"

"Right now? I'm going up to Suffolk for Christmas. Or do you mean with my life?"

"Well, both. Is that the people you were with last summer – where the man was killed?"

"Yes. Why?"

He squinted through his wine at the light. "Well, you know I told you at the time I wasn't altogether happy about that affair. Of course I've no authority over you, but naturally I feel, well, *in loco parentis*, a bit. Nice wine, don't you think?" He paused to drink.

"Delicious. So you don't approve of my going to Suffolk?"

"It's none of my business of course, but, since you ask me, no, I don't. For one thing, I hate to rub it in, but if you're thinking of getting a job, it wouldn't look too good as an address. There was a deplorable amount of publicity about that affair."

She made a face. "I see what you mean. Well, you don't need to worry because as a matter of fact I haven't the money for my fare. I was counting on getting my allowance today." Surprising how much the admission hurt her.

"Of course. I was expecting that, and of course we'll tide you over . . . no, no, don't thank me. Naturally the firm feels responsible in a way and we'll take care of you. But rushing off to Suffolk . . . well, that's something else again."

No use raging, as she once would have, at the iron hand so soon apparent. "What would you suggest? Of course I'll have to get a job as soon as possible, but there's not much chance before Christmas; it's only ten days." As she talked she was doing desperate sums in her head, trying to make the pitiful remains of her allowance stretch to the fare to Suffolk. Perhaps if she pawned something . . . her watch? Anything rather than be beholden to Paul Protheroe. And she would have to borrow from him if she stayed in London – hotels came expensive and there was no one she knew well enough to land on at such short notice. It was not the first time she had come up against the inconvenience of having no family. She had been on her own ever since she ran away from Featherstone Hall, years ago. She had got used to it, more or less, but it was certainly inconvenient now. Paul Protheroe was her nearest functioning relative and starvation would not make her go to stay with him. Or would it? she wondered, trying to find her way in a bleak new world.

He watched her cogitations for a minute, toying comfortably with his wine glass. When he saw her look of puzzlement deepen into one of distress, he spoke. "As a matter of fact I've got a suggestion to make – very tentative, and merely as a stop-gap – I thought of you when I heard about it, though I hardly like to suggest . . ." He paused and looked at her dubiously. There had been times in the past when his suggestions had been met with a vehemence he had not relished. But Patience was tamer now.

"I'll do anything," she said. "I'll have to. Two-thirds of an English degree's not going to get me anywhere. D'you know anyone who wants a good general maid? They're supposed to be in short supply aren't they?" She looked down at her elegant grey flannel suit. "I'm not sure these are quite the clothes for scrubbing floors, but never mind."

He laughed – how she had always disliked that smooth laugh. "Oh, well, I don't think it need be quite so bad as that. Though as things have turned out it is perhaps a pity

7

you insisted on college instead of that business course I – if you remember – recommended. But we won't talk about that now," he went on hastily as he noticed the red spot in each pale cheek, a sign, as he knew too well, that quiet Patience Smith was about to explode. "What I have to suggest," he went on, "is a good bit better than floor-scrubbing, though hardly glamorous, I'm afraid, and might mean a little eating of humble pie."

"Oh – glamour." She dismissed it. "But what do you mean about humble pie?"

"D'you remember old Mrs Ffeathers?"

"I should rather think I do. But is she really still alive? I thought she was about a hundred that gruesome time when I lived at Featherstone Hall after Father died."

"That's all to be forgotten," he told her. "Your running away. I have no doubt there was wrong on both sides. In my line of business you get used to that. And it's really an advantage now, because the old lady doesn't much like strangers, and she remembers you as having spunk, she says."

"The one that got away? And now she wants me back? But why?"

"For company."

"Company? But she's got all those children and grand-children – maybe great ones by now for all I know. What does she want company for? The Hall was so full of relations when I was there you couldn't see for cousins." How she had hated it, that houseful of lively extroverted Ffeatherses, when she went there in the first loneliness after her parents' deaths. It was no wonder she had lost touch with them since. Even now the memory rankled. But that was nothing if there was a job. "Have they all left home?" she asked.

"Oh, no, there are always plenty of people in the house, but Josephine Ffeathers is getting on now, and she needs a bit more, well, consideration, than her own family think of giving her. So for the last few years she's had a companion down there – or rather she's had a great many. I'll be honest with you, Patience, it's a difficult position. Mrs Ffeathers is apt to be a bit temperamental at times – she's over ninety, so perhaps she has a right to be – and then of course there are the family. I expect you remember what they're like."

"Yes." Patience managed to convey a great deal in her one syllable.

He made a vague gesture and turned it into a summons to the waiter. "Two coffees, please. Yes, I warned them it would be difficult, but they would insist on getting elderly women – oh, very nice, you know, quite unobjectionable, but I told them from the first it wouldn't work."

"And it didn't?" Like my going to college, she thought. What fools people are not to take Cousin Paul's advice. He's always right.

"No, it didn't. They had a trained nurse first. She stayed for a while, but then she said there wasn't enough for her to do – and of course she was quite right; there's not much wrong with Josephine Ffeathers' health – tonics, you know, proper care, but not much in it for a nurse. Then they had a succession of youngish old ladies and of course they bored poor Josephine to tears – stories of life with father at Cheltenham and whist drives in India fifty years ago – you know the kind of thing. You can imagine the effect it had on Josephine. You

may like her or not, but you can't get away from it; she
has lived."

"Yes, that's quite true." For once she found herself
sympathising with him, as she remembered the vehement,
raddled old lady who had so alarmed her at eleven.

"Well, either she got so bored she drove them out of the
house, or she shocked them so that they left on their own
account, poor things. The last one's just gone . . . Young
Josephine was in my office yesterday telling me all about it;
they're in despair it seems, with Christmas coming on and
a lot of arrangements of their own. The old lady's a glutton
for company these days, and I can see Josephine's afraid
she'll wreck the party. Anyway, I hope you don't mind, but
I did just mention your name to her. I thought it might be
something to tide you over – and after all, it isn't as if it
was strangers."

"No," said Patience, "it certainly isn't." Then, recognising
the ingratitude of her tone, she went on. "It was good of you
to think of me. What did Josephine – Mrs Brigance say?"

"She was all for it. She asked me to tell you she'd consider
it a personal favour if you'd come, and she'll do everything
to make it easy for you. But why don't you go over and talk
to her yourself? She's got to go back tonight, but she'll be at
the hotel this afternoon and is hoping you'll phone her." He
looked at his watch. "As a matter of fact I half promised I'd
get you to call her from here; she may be staying in for it."

"Oh," said Patience, "then I'd better. Will you excuse
me?"

"Of course." He rose and pulled back her chair before
the hovering waiter could reach it. "The telephone's on the
landing."

10

Desperate to get me off his hands, Patience thought. But one could hardly blame him. Very inconvenient to have one's clients left bankrupt on one . . . and the last straw when that client was a cousin. She had pressed Button B and heard her two pence drop into oblivion before she considered what she should say. The idea of Christmas at Featherstone Hall filled her with unmitigated gloom, but as Paul said, it would tide her over. And it would save her from having to borrow more money from him. A major consideration. "Mrs Brigance, please," she said to the hotel's chilly voice and was put through before she had time for further doubts.

"Patience" – Mrs Brigance's voice was richer than ever – "what a godsend to hear from you. Has Paul explained? You will come, won't you? It'll save our lives; I can't tell you how grateful we'll be. Mother'll be a different woman when she hears; she was always devoted to you, you know. It hurt her terribly when you vanished like that – but we won't say anything about that; the main thing is that you'll come. Can you come down with me tonight? That'd be too, too marvellous and we could get you settled in before Christmas – we've got swarms of people coming; you'll enjoy it. I'm taking the six o'clock. Be a lamb and angel and meet me on it – first class, of course – and we'll settle everything then."

She was silent at last, and Patience began to voice her own doubts with a hesitant, "But, Mrs Brigance, I'm not sure—" It was her longest contribution to their talk.

Mrs Brigance overwhelmed her with, "'Josephine', my dear ridiculous child, and don't say a word to me about not being sure. Of course at a time like this – I was so sorry to hear about it all from Paul – so thoughtless of your poor father – but of course you ought to be with your family, and if your family can make it worth your while to you, why, so much the better. Naturally if you hate us all, there's nothing to stop your leaving. Come on, there's a good child, give us a trial; we won't let Mother eat you, I promise. I expect Paul's been telling you how she bullied the poor old dodos we've been having for her. The wretch, I made him promise not to, but of course with you it'll all be quite, quite different, and I'll have Mark take special care of you. He was asking about you only the other day. D'you remember how you and he used to fight? You'll find him something else again these days – just down from Cambridge and Paul tells me you've been up at Oxford, bright young thing that you are." She paused for breath, but went on before Patience could gather her scattered wits. "Well, thank goodness that's settled, and I'll meet you on the six o'clock. D'you remember what I look like? It's ten years, isn't it, just think of that! Tall and dark and Mark says I don't look a day over thirty, but you mustn't believe everything he tells you . . . Oh, and a fur coat – Persian lamb this year, and oh my dear that reminds me, would you be a saint and angel and do something for me this afternoon? I've got a million phone calls to make – of course all the Christmas planning falls on me – and I've just remembered I was supposed to pick up my mink from Gogarty's – they've taken months to repair it, the brutes, but it's ready now, and if you could just drop in and collect it for me I'd love you for ever – and wear it for me, would you, there's a dear; I hate to have it packed up. I'll call them up and tell them you're coming for it, so there'll be no trouble."

"Your three minutes are up," said the exchange and Patience remembered, with a sinking of the heart, that she had no more coppers. And anyway, what was the use . . .

"That's wonderful," Josephine Brigance was saying. "I'll look for you, mink and all, on the six o'clock. Simply lovely to see you, my pet. Bye bye."

Patience emerged from the booth dazed as a deep sea diver surfacing and saw Paul waiting for her at the foot of the stairs. "All fixed?" he asked. "Splendid. I hope you don't mind; I've got to be getting along – client turning up at three and a lot of homework to get through first. Never a dull minute in our profession, I can tell you." He stood aside to let her pass first through the heavy revolving doors. "And now how about that little advance we were going to make you? D'you want to come along and pick it up? I'm afraid I'll have to be formal and make you sign for it, but it's only five minutes' walk."

"No, thanks very much." What a comfort to be able to say it. "It's very nice of you, but I'm going down to Featherstone Hall with Mrs Brigance tonight and I expect I can get an advance from her if it comes to it – but I hope it won't."

"You're sure you're all right for this afternoon? No Christmas shopping to do?"

"Nothing serious. There are some advantages about having no family, you see. No, I thought I'd go to a news theatre as a matter of fact – there is one round Oxford Circus somewhere isn't there? I promised Mrs Brigance I'd pick up her fur coat at Gogarty's and I'd like to leave that till the last thing – it seems a bit unsuitable to go swaggering about in mink all afternoon. Thank you so much for the lunch and all you've done." She was suddenly tired of keeping up appearances for Paul's benefit. After all, why bother? She held out her hand. "Let me know just how much I owe you, will you? I'm afraid it'll have to be on the instalment plan." On this practical note she left him and headed straight for her news theatre, where she sat for an hour staring not at the screen but at penury.

When she came out, she felt better. After all, she had a job, even if it could hardly be called an attractive one. And perhaps even that would not be so bad; perhaps all those cousins had mellowed with age. How she had hated them, Mark Brigance most of all. Turning into the side street that led to Gogarty's she almost ground her teeth as she remembered the misery he and his twin sister Mary had made of her life when she had stayed with them as a child. Mrs Brigance had not mentioned Mary, it occurred to her, but then Mark had always been her favourite. It was bad luck on Mary that Mr Brigance had not lived to take her part.

In her private crisis she had forgotten about Christmas, but there was no mistaking the good-humoured chaos inside Gogarty's. She hovered for a minute by a counter piled high with brilliant artificial flowers. Should she take down a present for old Mrs Ffeathers? She still had three pounds in her purse – quite enough for the fare down and a bunch of violets for an old lady's coat. But no – she pushed on through the crowd – a present for Mrs Ffeathers meant presents for everyone, and that was impossible, even if she had wanted to give presents to Mark and Mary and the others. She must establish herself at once and firmly on an employee basis, then the problem would never arise. She cast a longing eye on the glove department – she had meant to buy herself some, but they would have to wait – hurried through a crowd of anxious husbands at the costume jewellery counters and made her way into the comparative tranquillity of the fur department. A bored and elegant young woman was showing off inexpensive fur scarves for the benefit of yet another harassed male. Her companion, wearier still, drooped over to Patience. "Mrs Brigance's coat?" She became faintly animated at the name. "Oh, yes, we have it out for her. You'll wear it?" She picked a glossy three-quarter-length cape from a nearby rack and draped it over Patience's shoulders. "There, it suits you."

Patience laughed. "It needn't. I'm not going to be buying mink for a while."

"Me neither." The girl became almost human. "If you'll just sign here, please. I'm glad you came for it; don't tell Mrs Brigance, but it nearly got sold this afternoon. I'd been off the floor, see, and when I came back there was a customer trying it on, as pleased as punch. Said she thought of having herself one made like it when I told her it wasn't for sale. Nice work, if you can afford it."

"Yes, very," said Patience, turning away. As she did so, she became aware of a figure hovering in the background, apparently acting as audience to the exhibition of fur ties that was still going listlessly on. Surely there was something familiar . . . Of course. He had turned and was approaching her. She held out her hand. "How nice to see you, Mr Crankshaw."

Geoffrey Crankshaw shook her hand vigorously. "Nice to see you, Patience." He used the Christian name with obvious intent. "I hope you don't mind; I've been following you. I saw you in Gloves and wasn't sure it was you – but I wasn't taking any chances. I'm delighted to have run you to earth among the minks."

15

She laughed. "Not my mink, I'm afraid. How are you?"

"Thank goodness for that – Oh, very well, and you?"

"Thriving." How odd, she thought to herself, pausing in the exchange of banalities; that last time they had met they had been earnestly discussing the murder he had just solved with her help. "What are you doing these days?"

"Pounding a metropolitan typewriter mostly. I'm supposed to be cutting my teeth on routine at the Yard – and very dull most of it is, too. It's pure luck, thank God for it, that I'm here this afternoon – I'll bless Gogarty's shoplifter till my dying day. But, damn it, it means I can't even ask you to come out for a cup of tea – I'm very much on duty. When can I see you?"

"I'm afraid I'm going down to Sussex tonight – I'd love to have heard about Scotland Yard. Is it really so dull? I can't believe it – not after last summer." As they talked they had been making their way back towards the main entrance and now she paused to look at her watch. "Good lord, I must hurry; I'd no idea it was so late."

His face was as engagingly young as ever under fair hair, but there was a new firmness about his manner. "I know it's asking a lot," he said, "but couldn't you possibly think of an errand or two to keep you here till six? Then we could go out and have a drink somewhere."

"I'm awfully sorry" – she really was – "but I've got to catch a six o'clock train." She held out her hand. "It has been nice to see you again."

"Well, promise you'll call me up next time you're in town. Whitehall one-two-one-two, extension five-three-six."

"I ought to be able to remember that." She smiled at him. "I'll certainly ring you, but goodness knows when I'll be in town again. Goodbye." She turned and pushed her way through the heavy doors, furious with Josephine Brigance and her six o'clock train. As she emerged she felt a touch on her arm.

"Excuse me, miss," said the shabby little man who had stopped her. "Might I just have a word with you?"

"With me? Why?" Inconspicuous though he was, she was certain she had never seen him before.

"You're sure this is the one?" He turned to a girl who stood beside him.

"It's her all right. She pointed her out ever so careful, and anyway you couldn't miss that coat." Coatless herself, she shivered as she spoke, and Patience, looking at her neat black dress and white collar, realised that she must be one of the shop assistants.

The man spoke again: "I'm afraid I'll have to ask you to step into the manager's office for a minute, miss. If you'll just come along quietly there needn't be any unpleasantness about it." He began to shepherd her back towards the doors.

"But what on earth's it all about?" It seemed simpler to go with them, and Patience asked the question as she made her way back through the big doors. "Let go of my arm, please." Something in her voice made him give her a quick, unhappy glance and drop the hand with which he had grasped her elbow.

"All right, so long as you'll come quiet," he said. "We don't want any fuss in the shop."

The manager was a worried-looking man in too beautiful a grey suit. "Yes?" He looked from Patience to her companions.

"Got her for you." The shabby little man seemed to swell as he spoke. "I reckon you won't have to bother with the Yard. Red-handed, thanks to this young lady." The girl in black blushed and stammered something, but Patience interrupted her. "What on earth is all this about?" she asked. "I came here, because it seemed simpler than making a scene in the shop, but now I'd like to know what it means."

"Listen to her," said the little man admiringly. "Caught red-handed and lays it on like that. No wonder she's got away with it so long."

"Got away with what?" Patience was beginning to lose her temper.

"Want me to put it in words of one syllable, do you?" the little man asked. "Well, shoplifting, then, since you're so particular. Just feel in your left-hand pocket, if it's not too much trouble."

"Left-hand pocket? What on earth are you talking about? I haven't got any pockets. I think this has gone about far enough." She turned to the manager, who stood, silent and anxious behind his desk, watching the scene.

The little man looked faintly worried and turned to the girl. "In the cape," she said, "that's what she told me. The pocket of the cape."

Patience looked down at Josephine Brigance's lavish fur cape. Then she investigated. Yes, surprisingly enough, there were deep pockets in the side seams. She put her right hand in; nothing.

"The left-hand pocket, she said." It was the girl who spoke.

"Who's 'she'?" As she spoke, Patience put her hand in

the other pocket, gasped slightly and drew out a long string of pearls.

"There you are." The little man was triumphant. "What did I tell you? But I give it to her for acting; she had me scared there for a minute." He held out his hand for the pearls and Patience automatically gave them to him. "Yes, there's our ticket, all right. They're off your counter, aren't they, Miss Jones?" He handed them to the girl in black.

She looked at them and Patience saw the whisper of a puzzled frown cross her forehead. But what she said was definite enough. "Oh yes, they're from my counter all right."

"And no sales check on the ticket." The little man was enjoying himself now. "You might as well give over," he said to Patience, "we've got you clean."

She was beginning to realise the full unpleasantness of the situation. "Look," she turned to the manager who still stood, silent and grave behind his desk, "this is a ridiculous mistake. I don't know how those pearls got there, but I certainly didn't take them. It's not even my cape; I just picked it up in the fur department for my cousin."

The little man allowed himself a harsh laugh. "It's a treat to hear her," he said. "You'd better tell your story, Miss Jones."

The manager was looking more worried than ever. "Yes," he said, "I think we'd better hear what Miss Jones has to say."

"Well, it was like this." Miss Jones was somewhat abashed by her position. "I was ever so busy with a couple of gents after engagement rings, when this young lady comes up to me and says—"

"Just a minute," the manager interrupted her, "do you mean this young lady?" He indicated Patience.

"Oh, no, sir." She was amazed at his error. "Quite another young lady, tall and dark with a black coat and glasses. Anyway, she leans over the counter and says, 'Excuse me,' ever so nice and polite, 'I know it's none of my business,' she says, 'but I just saw a girl pinch a string of pearls from your counter. What d'you think I ought to do about it?' So of course I knew all the trouble there'd been about shoplifting, and the Yard being called in and all" – Miss Jones preened herself – "so I rang my bell quick as I could for Mr Parry and asked the young lady to wait and speak to him. But she said no, she'd a train to catch, but it was a young lady in a mink cape with straight fair hair – 'Look,' she says, 'there I see her now,' and pointed to this young lady who was just coming through Gloves with a gentleman. 'She put it in the left-hand pocket of her cape,' she said, 'a long string of pearls: I hope you catch her, but I must scoot.' Or something like that, and of course I couldn't make her stay, could I?"

"No, I suppose you hardly could," the manager said regretfully, "but it's a pity. Did you get her name and address?"

Miss Jones's face fell. "No," she said, "she scooted so quick I didn't have time to say 'Boo' – if you'll excuse me, sir."

Patience had been collecting her wits. "Look," she said, again to the manager, "there has been some mistake and I think I can prove it." She turned to the girl. "You say she pointed me out to you when I was coming out of the glove department with a . . ." she hesitated.

20

"That's right, miss, with a gentleman. Tall, he was, and fair."

"Yes," Patience said. "It was Mr Crankshaw. I believe he's here on business and he'll tell you I was with him from the time I picked this coat up in the fur department. I couldn't have put those pearls in the pocket. I can't think how they got there, but I couldn't have done it." Horrible to have to drag Crankshaw in, but better now than later. She stole an anxious look at her watch. Five fifteen; there should still be time to catch the six o'clock if all went well.

"Mr Crankshaw?" The manager looked surprised. "The policeman?"

"That's right," Patience relaxed into a smile. "He's a friend of mine." The look on her shabby little captor's face was almost worth the whole episode.

There was an uncomfortable silence as they waited for Crankshaw. The manager acknowledged Patience's changed position by offering her a chair, and sat down himself behind his desk, fidgeting with some papers. The little man – clearly the shop detective, thought Patience – and the salesgirl looked at each other unhappily and at Patience with obvious resentment. Then there was a knock at the door and Crankshaw appeared. "You wanted to see me, Mr Mallieson?"

"Yes." The manager wasted no time. "Do you know this lady?"

Crankshaw turned. "Why, hullo, Patience, what are you doing here? Been shoplifting?" Then he saw the shop detective and the drooping salesgirl. "Good lord, what is all this?"

The manager explained about the accusation of the

21

unknown young woman. "And now," he concluded, "this lady says she was with you from the time she picked up the coat in the fur department till the moment she left the shop. Is that right?" They all looked hopefully at Crankshaw.

"Quite right," said Crankshaw. "As a matter of fact, I first saw Miss Smith in the glove department, without the cape. I thought I recognised her, and followed her through to Furs to make sure. Then I waited while the assistant found her the cape and she put it on, and spoke to her as she came away. I was watching all the time." He blushed slightly. "She couldn't have put anything in the pockets."

"I didn't know there were pockets," Patience said, "till I put in my hand. I don't understand it at all." But she was no longer worried. Geoffrey Crankshaw was here; he would take care of the situation.

He did. "It's quite clear there's not the shadow of a case against Miss Smith," he said to the manager. "Not but that you were perfectly right to stop her." The detective cheered up slightly. "I'd like to know what the young woman who started it all was up to, though. Too bad you didn't get her name." The salesgirl wilted visibly and he consoled her. "Never mind, she'd probably have given a false one if you'd asked her. What d'you say she looked like?"

"Tall and dark," the girl repeated it, "and a black coat and glasses . . . I'm afraid I didn't notice much; I was that rushed at the time; but she spoke ever so nicely."

"Can you think of anyone who looks like that, who'd go to the trouble to play a practical joke on you?" Crankshaw asked Patience.

"Not a soul. And it's not my idea of a very brilliant joke either."

"No," he said thoughtfully. "No, it isn't. The cape was hanging on a rack in the fur department when you went for it, wasn't it, so I suppose anyone could have taken the pearls and slipped them into the pocket."

"Oh, goodness," Patience said.

"What is it? Been noticing things again?"

She laughed, ignoring the three listeners in this sudden reminder of their previous intimacy.

"Yes, I remember now. The girl said she was off the floor for a while and when she got back there was someone trying the cape on . . . she was frightfully disappointed when she heard it wasn't for sale and said she'd have to have one made like it."

"That's it," said Crankshaw. "That's how it would be done. Perhaps we should have a word with the girl from the fur department, Mr Mallieson. We'd better get this business cleared up as far as we can if you don't mind waiting a minute, Patience."

"Not a bit." He was very much in command, she thought.

Another awkward silence fell as they waited for the arrival of this new witness. It was broken, surprisingly, by the salesgirl. "You know," she said to no one in particular, "it's a funny thing; I could have sworn they cleared those long strands of pearls yesterday. There were a lot Tuesday when I was on but I'm sure I didn't notice any when I took over this morning."

"You were off yesterday, were you?" Crankshaw asked.

"Yes. One day off before Christmas for shopping. It comes in ever so handy." She looked at the manager a little anxiously.

A timid knock announced the salesgirl from the fur

23

department. She at once confirmed that the fur cape had been hanging on a rack at the side of the department since Mrs Brigance had called up about it. Mrs Brigance had particularly asked for it to be ready. Yes; she had come back on to the floor in the course of the afternoon and found a young lady trying the cape on . . . a tall dark young lady with glasses – very disappointed she'd been when she heard the cape was not for sale.

"Well, there you are," said Crankshaw, when she had been thanked and dismissed, "an obvious plant, but Lord knows why. You're sure you can't think of anyone with a grudge against you, Patience?"

"Not a soul. They must have mixed me up with someone else. Or could it be something to do with the shoplifting that's going on? To distract your attention or something?"

"That's an idea." The manager came to attention at once and looked at his watch. "Just on closing time too – always their best time. Perhaps we'd all better get back to our posts." At this cue the shop detective and the salesgirl, who had visibly been waiting for a chance, faded gratefully away. He turned to Patience. "I'm extremely sorry for the inconvenience we've caused you, Miss Smith, but you can see how it is; we've got to protect ourselves."

"Of course, I don't blame you a bit. But now I must rush, if it's all right; I've got a train to catch." Crankshaw held the door open for her, chafing at the necessity that constrained him to stay. "You must catch it?" he asked.

"Definitely: it's a job." And on this puzzling note she left him to attend somewhat absent-mindedly to his conference with the manager.

Two

Patience found Josephine Brigance snugly ensconced in her first-class carriage with the Persian lamb coat well in evidence on the rack. Looking at the mask of make-up that made do for a face, Patience thought it was just as well she had not had to rely on recognition alone. The Josephine she remembered had been a stalwart country dweller who had only just, and under protest, given up hunting and who still, regardless of her children, spent much of her time coaxing miracles out of the two or three depressed horses that were kept in the derelict stables of Featherstone Hall.

Times had certainly changed, Patience thought, surrendering herself to a highly perfumed embrace.

"Patience, my lamb, it's heaven to see you. You're an angel to come, and, bless you, you've got my cape. No, no, keep it on; it's cold in here – you'd think at least there'd be enough heating on a fast train – going to the dogs we are, my dear, and quickly, but at least you'll find things pretty comfortable at the Hall. We had central heating put in just after the war, you know, and it's wonderful how Joseph manages to get hold of coal to run it on – he has the most useful friends, the lamb. You remember Joseph, don't you, my pet?"

Patience remembered old Mrs Ffeathers' younger son with a minimum of enthusiasm as a red-faced man who did something in the City and came home smelling of beer to pinch little girls where they liked it least. "Yes, indeed," she said. "Does he still go up to town every day?"

"Good Lord, no. You are behind the times. He did wonderfully in the war one way and another and he's been resting on his laurels ever since."

"Really," Patience was amazed. "I'd have thought he was – " she hesitated, then braved it – "a bit old for the army."

"The army?" Josephine raised enamelled eyebrows. "Who said anything about the army? No, no, the home front, my dear, the home front. Supplies and buildings and all those things – he made a packet, I can tell you. You should see Emily in her pearls."

"How is Emily?" Patience had forgotten all about Joseph's insignificant wife, probably because everyone else always did.

"Oh, pale as ever. I wanted her to come up with me this time and get something done about her face – really, my dear, you should see it – too dreary – but she said Joseph was satisfied with her the way she was . . . of course he is, never looks at her from month's end to month's end. Lucky she's got that fish-faced girl to keep her occupied. Lord, you should hear Mark on his cousin Priss – she wanted to be a social worker, would you believe it! A Ffeathers a social worker! Mother put her foot down pretty hard about that, I can tell you. Poor old Priss; if you ask me it was anything to get away from the Hall. She fell with a crash for Mark – they all do, my lamb, they all do – and of course he'd as soon take

26

out an earwig." She paused and lit another cigarette. "But tell me all about yourself, my sweet; Paul says you're quite the young intellectual these days, but you look all right, thank God. I was prepared for the worst when he said that. Mary wanted to go to Girton while Mark was up, but I wasn't having any of that; just spoiling your market, that's what it is. You'll live to be thankful you didn't finish; what in the name of goodness does a girl want with a lot of phoney education? Just tell me that."

Patience did not try. "What is Mary doing?" she asked.

"Getting in and out of engagements so fast I've lost count," said her mother proudly. "You must have seen pictures of her in the columns. She's got a flat in town now but she'll be down for Christmas. She's bringing a friend – such a charming young man – Tony Wetherall. He actually has a job – public relations or something for one of the papers; I never remember which, but it works out beautifully. He has tickets for everything, my dear; Mary adores it. They are going to the opera tonight or she'd have come down with us, but I'm delighted to have a chance to hear all about you before we get down to that madhouse. I do hope you'll be happy, my pet. Mother's a bit difficult at times, but all she needs is handling. I know you're just the person for it, and the trouble is the rest of us have such a lot on our plate these days it's hard to find the time . . . God knows how I'm going to get through this Christmas – you'll have to be an angel and help out with the housekeeping; I'm sure you're wonderful and Mary's no earthly use – far too busy looking after her complexion. Not that I blame her; after all, a girl's face is her fortune, isn't it? I'm so glad you turned out so nice-looking, my dear; I always told Mother that puppy fat wouldn't last. She was in despair about you, poor Mother, and of course we hadn't the money to take you in hand."

Much to Patience's relief, Josephine ended her monologue at this point by getting out *Country Life* and devoting herself systematically to its contents. She was free at last to stare out of the window into the moving darkness and brood about the disconcerting happenings of the day. She had practically got used to being penniless by now, the shock of that having been lost in the still greater one of almost being arrested. Who? she asked herself over and over again. And why? She had got no further than this, though almost an hour had passed, when Josephine roused her. "Only five minutes to Leyning," she said. "Mark is meeting us with the station wagon, the dear thing. Be prepared to be bowled over, my dear. Oh, by the way" – she was busy applying a new layer to the mask of make-up – "about salary; you'll have to talk to Mother. She still holds the purse-strings – and pretty damned tight, too, I can tell you. You'd better be firm with her, the old skinflint." Disconcertingly, those were the first genuine-sounding words Josephine had spoken.

If Patience was not bowled over by Mark Brigance, she was pleasantly surprised. The disagreeable and bullying little boy she remembered with such dislike had turned into a young man whose black Byronic handsomeness would have been formidable if his manner had not been so friendly. In the course of taking their bags and shepherding them into the car, he made Patience feel that there was a strong and pleasant bond of cousinship between them that she had totally forgotten. Any minute, she thought, they would be talking about the good old days.

In fact, Mark and his mother were busy with an almost unintelligible interchange of family gossip on the front seat. She caught a few phrases: "Mary and Tony Wetherall on Saturday night . . . Gran had another tantrum this morning . . . What do we do about Christmas boxes? . . . Uncle Seward's blasted piano . . ."

This, very emphatically from Mark, reminded Patience that Josephine had told her nothing about her older brother and his family. Seward had decided at an early age that he was a pianist of genius. His mother's determined opposition had merely confirmed him in his belief, and it was only after he had run away from home to take up his career that the horrid truth of capable mediocrity had come home to him. He had struggled on for some years until the combination of an ailing wife and four children too close together became too much for him and he staged a prodigal's return, though there were more husks than veal in his reception. Still, his mother had taken him in, had even allowed him to give piano lessons to all her grandchildren and had borne with his discovery of latent genius in each one in turn. Encouraged by her more comfortable circumstances, his wife Grisel had remained an invalid dwindling on to a sofa – almost, it would seem, in competition with her mother-in-law, had that energetic old lady allowed such a thing in her house. Of the four children who had originally precipitated the return, two – the most talented two, their father maintained – had shortly afterwards died in an epidemic of diphtheria, leaving a girl and boy, Leonora and Ludwig, in an unhappy minority among their cousins. Priss could always be relied on to side with Mark and Mary; Leonora and Ludwig had to conform or go to the wall. Patience well remembered with what an ill grace they had conformed, and wondered, as Mark steered the station wagon deftly through Leyning, what further vicissitudes of their career were covered by Josephine's significant silence.

Leaving Leyning, the car began to climb the long slope of the South Downs. "Too bad you're getting back at night, Patience," Mark said over his shoulder. "I remember how you loved this view."

Again Patience was surprised at the veil of friendliness he managed to cast over their previous relationship. "Nice of you to remember," she said.

"Of course I remember. We'll walk over to the Great Crossroad tomorrow and you shall see the sea again – they've cleared the woods along the edge and you can see clear to the Isle of Wight."

"We'll have to see about tomorrow." Josephine sounded faintly impatient. "Mother may not want to spare Patience so soon, now she's got her back at last."

Patience shivered slightly. Suddenly she remembered the spider effect of old Mrs Ffeathers, sitting at the heart of her house, queen of the web, and allowing none of her children to escape. Was the same true of the grandchildren, she wondered? And were the silken meshes already preparing for her?

She was tired and morbid, she thought, and saw with relief that the car was turning in at the great gates of Featherstone Hall. By the light of the headlamps she saw with surprise that those gates, and the pillars from which they hung, no longer stood up by a miraculous concession of gravity. The loose and decaying stones had been replaced, the heavy balls on which she had so often played 'I'm the king of the castle'

– only she never was; it was always Mark – were back on top of the gateposts. Even more than Josephine's prosperous conversation, this made her realise what an improvement there must have been in the once depressed fortunes of the Ffeathers. What would old Mrs Ffeathers be like in prosperity, she wondered, if even poverty had left her a successful tyrant?

The car stopped outside the porticoed front door and she soon had further opportunity to notice the improvement in the family's circumstances. The big, shabby, comfortless downstairs hall had been transformed into something out of *House and Garden*; not, she thought, looking round at the pastel and aluminium furnishings, that it was in the least more comfortable.

A musical-comedy maid to match the furnishings appeared in the far doorway. "Mrs Ffeathers is in her room," she told Josephine. "She's expecting you." Nothing had changed, thought Patience, no one else mattered.

Josephine dropped her fur coat on a glass seat. "Back to the dungeon," she said. "Come on, Patience."

Mark laughed. "Good luck, Cinderella," he said, taking the mink cape, "do your stuff, there's a good girl. You've no idea how this family needs a scapegoat. But don't let the old tartar get you down; we're all on your side. I'll have a nice big drink all ready for you when you come down."

"I wouldn't be surprised if Mother wanted Patience to have supper with her tonight," said Josephine repressively, but Mark was not to be quelled.

"Not her," he said. "She's feeling so much better today she thinks she'll eat with her dear children . . . so leave that frontless dress in the closet, Mama, acushla, and out with the black velvet and pearls."

Pearls, thought Patience, following Josephine up the big central stairway, pearls. Who? Why? A tall dark girl with glasses . . . the world was full of them. She shook herself, and followed Josephine Brigance into the big bedroom that faced the head of the stairway. Here, nothing had changed. The room was still heavy with red velvet – full-length curtains of it over the three high windows along the front of the house and a dark crimson corner where stood a huge four-poster bed also hung with it. Taking this in at a glance, Patience crossed the room to the fireplace where old Josephine Ffeathers sat throned in her huge, red, wing-backed chair, her imperious profile silhouetted against its dark background as she turned sharp eyes on Patience. "Well, so you've come back at last." It was not said unkindly. "Lost all your money, I hear, and a good thing too. Money never did young people any good – it's when you get to be an old hag like me you need it. That's what I keep telling my children, but they won't listen. But they'll learn; you'll all have to learn." She noticed Josephine hovering in the doorway. "What are you hanging around for? I didn't ask for you, did I? I want to have a talk with Patience – alone, you understand." Her voice was raised into the angry bark Patience remembered so well. Then, as the door closed silently behind Josephine she broke into charming and conspiratorial laughter. "She takes it from me," she said to Patience, "they all take it from me. They have to. But you ran away and never came back – and I believe I'm going to have to forgive you. You look just like your mother – grandmother, I mean. But what are you doing

standing on one leg in the corner like that? Come here and
kiss me and then pour us a glass of sherry, there's a good
child." It was an approximation to the bark she had used to
Josephine, but Patience found it unnecessary to resent it. She
kissed the highly polished old cheek and poured the sherry
silently. "You haven't got much to say for yourself, have
you?" said Mrs Ffeathers. "Don't forget you're supposed
to be here to amuse me. That'll be a weight off their minds
downstairs; they draw lots every night for whose turn it is
to sit with Grandma and think I don't know it." She took
a hearty pull at the sherry. "But I'll surprise 'em, one way
or another. I've not changed much, have I?" She darted a
quick inquisitorial look at Patience. "Don't lie; I'll know if
you do; I've had enough practice."

Patience looked at her. "No, you haven't changed a bit,"
she said. "Your hair's a bit whiter, and you don't frighten
me as much as you did, but otherwise I don't see any
difference at all."

"Used to frighten you, did I?" The old woman was vastly
pleased. "So that's why you ran away. I always wondered.
My one failure. Or were you my one success? The others
never ran – or not far – and look at them now. You know
about Seward! Concert pianist, he wanted to be. I gave him
a chance – music lessons and all found; and then I listened
to him; didn't need to do more. Concert pianist! But of
course he wouldn't believe me; flounced off to prove it to
me . . . He proved it all right; wait till you see him, poor
Seward, and Ludwig and Leonora." She made an eloquent
face. "Sometimes I think our sins do come home to roost,
when I look at my grandchildren, but you'd think they'd
have more blood in them." She emptied her glass. "Oh,

yes, Mark and Mary are lively enough – and Josephine's my own child . . . But trust them? Good God! Take my advice, my girl, and look where you're going in this house; you'll need to. They never did a charitable thing in their life, and if they tell you they're doing you a favour having you here, just remember, it's the first they ever did. And now, about salary. Josephine said she'd left me to discuss it with you – nice of her, considering I sign all the cheques in this house." She laughed at Patience's surprised expression. "I acted Cordelia once – disagreeable young woman – but you'll never catch me doing a Lear. I thought Josephine had a particularly Goneril look tonight, come to think of it; she hasn't been hatching anything with you, has she?"

"Hatching anything? What do you mean?"

"Oh, almost anything. Offering you some arsenic to put in my tea, suggesting that the old are better painlessly out of the way – anything like that. Don't look so shocked, my poor girl, it's time you grew up. Twenty-one aren't you? Nobody told you the facts of life yet? Well, it's time you learned. I'm an old woman and nobody wants me around, but I'm enjoying myself and I'm not going to hurry for anyone. I shall pay you four pounds a week, with keep, of course, and tomorrow I shall make a will leaving everything to you. That'll make you behave."

"But you can't – I don't want you to—" Patience began to protest, but was interrupted.

"Of course I can, and of course you want me to," said old Mrs Ffeathers. "It's left to the fifty-two letter alphabet at the moment – more fun than dogs' homes, don't you think? But I don't see why you shouldn't have a run for your money. They all have, and they've all been cut off, and they know it. When I die they won't have a penny; not one of them. That's why I'm alive today. And now I think it's time we went down to dinner. I'm sure you must be longing to meet your darling cousins – remember, you were *so* devoted to them." The mimicry of her daughter was perfect. "Give me your arm, my dear, I find the stairs a little trying. Don't you worry; I'll get four pounds' worth of work out of you."

The rest of the family were already assembled at the long dinner table when Mrs Ffeathers made her entrance on Patience's arm. "You've met all my zoo," she said. "I shan't bother to introduce them, they're not worth the trouble. I expect you'll be able to work out which is which. Here's Patience," she said to the table. "You're not to make her life a misery to her. I want her to stay. If she's to be made unhappy I'll do it myself. And I think it only fair to tell you that I'm making a will in her favour tomorrow. Josephine, you must call up Paul Protheroe after dinner. I want him down here first thing tomorrow to draw it up for me. Mark, what's so funny?"

Mark let his suppressed chuckle come to the surface. "You didn't take long this time, did you, Gran? I thought you'd get tired of that alphabet pretty quick. You can't bully fifty-two letters, can you?"

"You're an impertinent young ruffian." Mrs Ffeathers' voice was amused. Then it changed. "Stop that sniggering, Priscilla, or I shall have to ask you to leave the room; if you can't behave like a grown-up you're much better back in the nursery."

"I'm sorry, Granny." Priss's colourless face turned scarlet under the limp, mouse-coloured hair.

"And don't call me Granny. Ugh; smelling salts and

35

lavender water and church twice on Sundays. Didn't your father ever tell you what I was when I was young?" She paused menacingly, and Priss was forced to reply.

"An actress." She blushed more hotly than ever.

"Good; an actress. And did he tell you who left me all the money you're all pining after so? Tell me that." She waited, beady eyes fixed on Priscilla, who looked as if she was praying for the earth to open and swallow her. Beside her, her mother, an even more faded blonde, opened her mouth like a fish, closed it again and looked appealingly at her husband, who faced his mother from the foot of the table.

Joseph ignored the look and burst into a hearty laugh. "Not much sense of shame about you, is there, Ma? I'm not sure the nursery *isn't* the best place for the children when you come down to meals. You've shocked your protégée, too. Don't worry, Patience, you'll get used to it; we all have. And at any rate, the money's there; you oughtn't to complain of its being left to you." He seemed to find this a great joke. It was odd, Patience thought, but none of them seemed in the least put out by the announcement about Mrs Ffeathers' will; in fact she thought she had caught a look of actual pleasure on Josephine's face. But presumably these changes were everyday affairs in this curious household.

She looked down the long table. Mrs Ffeathers was cross-examining Josephine about everything she had done, and every penny she had spent in London, while Mark, who sat between them, put in an occasional semi-comic remark in his mother's defence. Beyond Josephine, Priss and her mother Emily were concentrating pallidly on their turbot. Seward tapped out a dreary tune on the tablecloth with his fork, while Joseph shouted at his sister-in-law,

Grisel, who was visibly regretting that she had left her invalid couch and come down to dinner. Between her and Patience sat her two children, Ludwig and Leonora, deep in a technical conversation about the treatment of fowl pest. Ludwig made a perfunctory attempt to include Patience in this, but when her ignorance became too obvious he gave her up in despair and turned back to his sister. Patience was glad of the chance to sit quietly and watch the others. They had not really changed much. Joseph was a little fatter, a little more boisterous, but she was sure he still pinched little girls when he got the chance. His wife had faded a little further to make up for his exuberance. Poor Priss was just the same white mouse as ever, and Ludwig and Leonora had always been a helpless satire on their own romantic names.

Mark leaned across the table to her. "Taking stock?" he asked. "How do you find us? The same lot of so-and-sos you ran away from? Or do we mellow with age?"

She smiled back at him. "Definitely, you mellow." And it was true, she thought; she really would not have known Mark.

Mrs Ffeathers had risen. "I shall expect you gentlemen for coffee in ten minutes." She led a silent procession of females through into the big drawing room and established herself in the chair nearest the fire. "Come here, Patience, and tell me how you lost your money. You didn't let Paul Protheroe invest it for you, did you? I wouldn't trust that young man an inch further than I could see him."

"No," Patience said, "it was in trust—"

She was interrupted by Josephine. "Really, Mother, I think you're very unfair to poor Paul. You know he's

37

worked like a slave for you, coming down here in season and out of season and making new wills."

"Hmm," said Mrs Ffeathers, "so it's 'poor Paul', is it? He's young enough to be your son, Josephine, and if you forget it, I'll take care to remind him. You've killed one husband, and that's enough."

"Mother, what are you saying?" Even from old Mrs Ffeathers this appeared to be more than Josephine could take.

"Well, nagged him into his grave then. I didn't know you were setting up for such a sensitive plant, my angel." Again the parody of Josephine's intense manner. "But where's my coffee? Priss, go and tell Mrs Marshland I want it at once and if it's not strong enough I'll fire her. That girl of yours is no use for anything but errands," she told Emily as the door closed on Priss. "Perhaps you'd better send her off to be a prison wardress or whatever it is she wants, after all. She depresses me, drooping about the house all day."

Emily sat up straighter in her chair. "Oh Mother, if you'd only let her; you've no idea what a difference it would make . . ."

"Don't call me 'Mother'," said Mrs Ffeathers. "Thank God, you're no child of mine; I'm not going to be held responsible for my sons' bad taste. And I don't know what you mean about my 'letting' Priss. I never did anything to stop her, did I? She's free to leave the house tomorrow if she wants to. I never asked one of you to live here and I don't see why you should expect me to pay you to go away."

"But the training" – Emily had drooped back into her chair – "it's so expensive, and you can't get anywhere without it."

"I never expected Priss to get anywhere – and she's not going to have my well-earned money to help her on her way. You tell her to go out and marry some poor fool; it's the only way she's ever going to come by money honestly – and I don't think it's very likely. Ah, here's my coffee; pour it out, Patience, there's a good child." The change in her tone when she turned to Patience was almost comic. But of course, Patience reflected, she had been an actress.

'Well-earned money'; her mind dwelt on the phrase. The legacy Mrs Ffeathers had spoken about at supper must account for the great change in the family's fortunes, for Patience had soon dismissed Josephine's hints about Joseph's success in the black market as idle boasting – or at least if he had made money, he must have lost it again as easily, or he would never be at home with his wife and family, let alone his mother. No, old Mrs Ffeathers' legacy was the secret, and Patience had heard enough hints about her sudden success on the stage and equally sudden disappearance from it to have a pretty good idea where it had come from. Rather comic, she thought, to have Mrs Ffeathers' highly respectable children struggling for it so visibly. But it was to be left to her tomorrow. She must catch Paul on his way in and make him refuse to draw up the will – not, of course, she added to herself, on moral grounds.

"Patience has made up her mind." Mrs Ffeathers' voice broke in on her thoughts. "Not going to take the dirty money, are you? But you'll find it feels just as good in the purse. And don't let them fool you; I worked for it, just as hard as you're going to for your four pounds a week; and very much the same way, if you come right down to it. But here come the men; we mustn't shock them."

She waited until everyone's cup was filled and then struck her hand suddenly on the table in front of her. "Now," she said, "you're all here, and I want to know who took five pounds out of my purse this morning. I left it in here for five minutes when I was doing the ordering with Mrs Marshland, and when I got back, someone had been at it. Now, out with it, who was it?"

There was an appalled silence. Then Joseph spoke up. "But are you quite sure, Mother? Money goes so fast these days, mightn't you have just thought . . ."

"Just thought!" She almost spat it at him. "You think because I'm ninety-one I'm getting senile, but you'll find you're mistaken. I know a five pound note when I've got it and I had three in my purse when I left it in here this morning." She looked round the room. "You all look as guilty as sin, so that's no help. And one of you's as bad as another, so nor's that, but I warn you this has got to stop and stop now. I've given you your allowances – good ones; I've stood for your scrounging a little of this and a little of that; I've paid your bills when they're reasonable; but petty thievery I will not have. If whoever took it doesn't return it to me personally tonight, there'll be no allowance cheques on the first of January. I won't turn you out of the house – you're my family, heaven help me – but you'll have to stay at home and take what's put before you. And very good for you too. Now, I'm going up to my room. I shall sit up till eleven and I expect my five pounds back before I go to bed. Good-night."

There was a horrified silence until the door had closed behind her. Then they all began to talk at once. "Lucky you" – Mark had settled beside Patience – "you're out of

40

it. Lord, I hope she returns it. I'm through if my cheque doesn't turn up on the first."

"She?" Patience asked.

He laughed. "That's right, stand up for your sex; but I'm betting on Priss. Just look at her."

"Just look at any of you," said Patience.

"And you on your monument, smiling at us. Never mind, it'll be your turn soon enough. She's a natural born torturer, old Gran. Come to think of it, I bet she never lost the blasted five quid. It's probably just her idea of how to make this the merriest Christmas of our little lives. Hold on, Uncle Joseph's going to orate."

Joseph cleared his throat and stood up in front of the fire. "This," he said, "is a very unfortunate situation and I can only hope for all our sakes that whoever was so ill-advised as to – er – borrow Mother's five pounds will return it at once." His 'chairman-of-the-meeting' manner deserted him all of a sudden. "God knows what'll become of us otherwise," he ended. "Mother means it, every word of it, you can see that."

Josephine looked at her watch. "Nine o'clock," she said. "Two hours to go. Don't you think it would be a good idea for us all to go up to our rooms? It would make it easier for – er – whoever it is to get up to Mother's."

"Damn good idea, Jo." Joseph sounded relieved. "Not much pleasure sitting round here like a bloody funeral anyway. Lovely Christmas we'll have if the money's not returned." He turned savagely to his wife. "And if you think I'm going to spend my last penny buying drinks for that nincompoop you've asked down for Priss, you've got another guess coming. She'll just have to catch him dry."

Emily and Priss shrank a little further into their remote corner while Josephine took her brother up. "It's early days to be worrying about Christmas," she said. "Let's worry about tonight first. All of us to our rooms and stay there and for God's sake take it back." She spoke to the room at large. "Good-night."

Three

Next day, black gloom fell on Featherstone Hall. Immured in her room, old Mrs Ffeathers let it be known that the five pounds had not been returned and her threat would be carried out. The party broke at once into dismal little family groups. Hostile looks were exchanged over shoulders, voices sank to a whisper when members of another group passed. Out of it all, Patience was to all intents and purposes in Coventry and was actually relieved when a maid summoned her to Mrs Ffeathers' room.

The old lady was propped up among pillows in the huge four-poster. "I never get up till after lunch," she replied to Patience's enquiry. "It's not worth the trouble. Though it almost would have been to see their faces this morning. How are they taking it? Hating each other already? I'm almost glad no one returned the money. It's going to be a very interesting Christmas, I can see."

"But you won't really do it?" Patience asked.

"What? Stop their allowances? I certainly will, and they know it. That's why they hate each other so this morning. I wouldn't want to be the fool who took it; they'll have it out of them before Christmas, I promise you that. I won't need to stop the allowances. Slow torture, that's what it'll be." The old lady said it with obvious relish.

Patience was appalled. "But haven't you any idea yourself who took it?" she asked. "It seems so unfair on the others."

"Not the slightest." Mrs Ffeathers was obviously pleased about it. "Anyone could have been into the drawing room while I was down in the servants' hall. I knew they'd come to it in time."

"You don't mean . . ." A horrid idea struck Patience. "You don't mean you left your bag about on purpose?"

The old lady chuckled hoarsely among her pillows. "Accidental done a' purpose, if you like. Just a little experiment. After all, I support them, don't I? I've a right to know what they're like. They'd take the pennies off a dead man's eyes, and you turn mealy-mouthed over a little experiment like that."

"But only one of them," Patience urged again. "It's so hard on the others. And you must have some idea . . ."

"Not a bit of it," said Mrs Ffeathers. "They'd any of them steal if they thought they could get away with it; the only question is who's fool enough to think I don't know how much money I've got. I'm rather betting on Priss myself – and if it's her the others'll wear her down in no time. We'll have a confession – or as good as – before Christmas, I promise you that. Now, get me my tonic, there's a good girl. I want to be at my brightest and best for this Christmas party. I wouldn't miss it for worlds. Emily's asked 'such a suitable young man' down for Priss. Brian Duguid of the best Salvation Army stock – poor young idiot offered her another cup at a charity tea and Emily's not had her claws out of him since. And Mary's Tony Wetherall's coming – I'm looking forward to meeting him; she can pick them, that girl. Her only trouble is she can't keep them. But she'll have a pretty good try with young Tony, when she hears her allowance is stopping. Josephine tells me he's got a good bank balance and a good job and no parents – perfect, isn't it? Josephine doesn't lie to me when she knows I'll find her out, so I believe all that. You'd better keep away from Tony if you want your eyes left in. I wouldn't put anything past Mary when her blood's up."

"Who's Mark having down?" Patience regretted the question as soon as it was spoken.

The old lady's bright eyes snapped. "Got your eye on him already, have you? Well, I don't blame you. And you shouldn't have much trouble, either, not once my will's changed. But I warn you, he's not the marrying type; he just might for the money, but he wouldn't enjoy it, and nor would you. You have your fun with him, while the going's good, and more power to you, but be sure you're the one that leaves him at the post. That's the way to do it; light and easy and lots of breath left for the next one." She paused and looked at Patience. "Well? Aren't you shocked?"

"Not a bit," Patience said truthfully. "I'm fascinated. I wish you'd tell me more." She paused, uncertain of her ground.

"About my wicked youth?" Mrs Ffeathers sat up straighter in bed and smoothed her hair with a well-ringed hand. "Perhaps I will one day. At least you don't blush and stutter like Priss and Leonora."

Another experiment, thought Patience, and on her this time. Oh, well; it must be dull to be old.

"If you start feeling sorry for me, I'll disinherit you." Mrs Ffeathers was a disconcertingly accurate mind-reader.

Patience laughed. "You can't. You haven't left it to me yet. And besides, I don't want it. I meant to ask you not to; I'd much rather you left it to those fifty-two letters. I'm sure they need it more than I do."

"You wait a bit; you'll find it's another story when it's been left you for a while. When you've started counting all the clothes you'd be able to buy, and the places you could go . . . you'll be on your knees to me yet, begging me not to cut you off. And I won't, not if you're good; I like you, Patience, you've a mind of your own. Now, run along and amuse yourself; I've got to get ready for Paul Pry Protheroe. How d'you like your precious cousin? No better than I do? That's good. Off with you and go to work on Mark. He's worth some trouble."

But Patience's only idea was to avoid the rest of the household. She longed to get out on to the downs by herself. Her room was next door to old Mrs Ffeathers' with a communicating door. She collected walking shoes and an overcoat, went quietly downstairs and let herself out of a side door that led almost directly to the great sweep of the hills. The air was cold and clear, wonderfully reviving after the overheated house, with its much boasted central heating and closed windows.

She climbed quickly, trying to tidy her mind. How long could she possibly keep this job? She must write off at once to her college to see if there was any possibility of getting a loan to cover her last two terms. Intolerable to contemplate more than a few weeks of Featherstone Hall and Mrs Ffeathers' experiments. She had a nasty feeling that she had been cast as the subject of the old lady's next bit of vivisection. There was too much feeling in those words, 'You'll be on your knees to me yet, begging me not to cut you off.' She really meant it. She thought her money could buy anything. Well, Patience thought, no kneeling for her, and with luck she'd be cut off pretty quickly and the whole uncomfortable episode would be over.

As the white road curved over the summit she paused and drew a deep breath, half of exhaustion, half of delight at the wide familiar view over the plain to the sea and beyond that to the mirage of the Isle of Wight. Maddening that the main road ran along this crest. It was impossible not to resent the parked car with its invisible occupant.

But at that moment the door of the scarlet roadster opened and Mark hailed her. "I thought you'd be coming up here," he said. "Didn't you promise to let me show you your view for the first time? It's unfair to scoot off by yourself like that. I never saw such a pace up the hill – did you think the devil was after you? You can see I didn't even try, just whistled for old Lizzy and here we are." He gave the car a proprietary pat on its bonnet. "Come into Leyning with me and meet Mary. I promised I'd fetch her. And I'm glad of a chance to get away from the Inquisition down there, I can tell you."

"Is it still going on?" Patience asked.

"Good Lord, yes. It's only just started. It'll go on till someone's nerve breaks. Gran knows what she's doing, the old fiend. Don't let her get her claws into you, Patience; she'll try, I promise you."

"How do you mean? She's been awfully nice to me so far." Patience felt honour bound to defend Mrs Ffeathers.

"Of course; she always is at first. But she can't stand having people free of her. We're no fun at all, of course, because she knows we'd be stuck without her money; but she has to have everyone in her power, and it's getting them there that amuses her. You watch out, Patience, I tell you."

Patience laughed. "Aren't you being rather melodramatic?"

"Haven't you been at Featherstone Hall long enough to see that melodrama is our daily bread? Gran couldn't live without it, and when it doesn't provide itself, she cooks it up, great Dracula dollops of it. Lord, I wish Christmas was over."

When they got to Leyning station he left Patience in the car. "Do you mind? They're brutes about parking here – they won't mind if you can move her on. We won't be a minute; the train's due."

In fact it drew in as he reached the platform gates and he had the pleasure of watching his sister catch sight of him and gracefully detach herself from the young man who was carrying her tiny bag.

"Another pick-up?" He did not kiss her.

She laughed. "I don't pick them up. They just happen. And he did ogle me so all the way from Clapham Junction I hadn't the heart to snub him. How are things at Hell Hall?"

"Hellish. Gran's on the war-path; I'll tell you all about that later. No time now; I've got Patience in the car."

"Have you so! That's quick work. I never thought she'd come."

"Oh, yes, Mother managed that all right. And Gran's

taken one of her fancies for Patience. Believe it or not, she's changed her will already, or as near as dammit."

"And you've got Patience in your car? Nice work. What's she like?"

"A surprise. You'll see. I'm not sure I'm not going to rethink things a bit. Stand by to give me a hand, Mar?"

"I sure will. But hadn't we better get along to her? And don't forget, if I pitch in for you there, you've got to show a hand for me with Tony. He's so damned upper-crust I sometimes wonder if I'll ever make the grade. I hope to God Christmas goes all right; I was crazy to ask him down."

"Yes, you were." Mark was telling her about the missing five pounds when they reached the car.

Back at the Hall Mrs Ffeathers was ending her interview with Paul Protheroe. "I want it ready to sign tomorrow," she said. "Your clerk can bring it down. It's no more pleasure for me to have you here than it is for you to come, and I don't want you ogling the girls any more than I can help." She pulled vigorously at the bell rope that hung by her chair and at the sound Josephine appeared from the hall where she had been hovering.

"Ah, there you are," said Mrs Ffeathers. "I didn't think you'd be far away. Take Paul downstairs and give him a drink and don't ask him more questions than you can help. Not that I care; you know what I was going to do and I've done it. Goodbye, Paul; I hope I don't have to see you again for a while."

"She's really doing it?" Josephine asked when the door was safely closed behind them.

"Yes, indeed. It may turn out to have been a lucky day for Patience when she came down here."

"Well, yes," Josephine said, "but you know how Mother is; she'll make fifty more wills before she dies. She's strong as a horse, Dr Findlayson says."

"She must be. Though mind you, I didn't think she looked quite so hearty this time as I've seen her; you'd better see she doesn't get too worked up over Christmas. It's often the outsiders who see the change, you know."

"Worked up over Christmas," Josephine laughed. "You don't know the half of it." She told him about the missing five pounds.

He lingered over his drink and presently she began to look impatiently at her watch. "Don't worry about me," he said. "I'll let myself out." When he was alone, he put down his glass, got up and left the room. He knew the house well enough to find his way to the door he wanted unobserved.

"Come in," called Priss to his knock. "There you are at last. I was beginning to think you hadn't made it."

He kissed her, like one who did it often and automatically. "I had a bit of trouble with Josephine. She would talk. Funny thing, though, she pretended to be furious, but I believe she's pleased the old lady's left her money to Patience. But to hell with her! How's my angel?"

"Not too bad. Have you heard about Christmas, though? I could scream."

"You mean the five pounds?"

"Oh, no, not that; that's just another of Gran's carry-ons. She'll find out who did it easy enough. No. Mother's asked that poisonous Brian Duguid down, 'so we can make better friends'. Isn't she the end?"

"Serves you right for saying you were going to Salvation Army meetings all those times. I told you it was asking for trouble. Your mother's such a hard-working woman, she was bound to make the most of it. But I'm not sure Brian might not be very useful this Christmas. Listen . . ." They talked for some time and then he looked at his watch. "Good Lord, I've been here half an hour. I hope to goodness nobody spots me going out."

"They won't; not if you go by the back way. Nobody uses it. When'll I see you?"

"Not till after Christmas, I'm afraid. We can't risk spoiling everything . . . You do your best with young Brian, my girl, and we'll be out of the wood in no time." He kissed her and left by the back way where, contrary to expectation, he met Leonora.

"Hullo," she said, "are you lost?"

"I am that. I thought they put in a downstairs lavatory when they did over the house."

"Of course they did. It's down the hall on the right."

She returned to the big workroom she shared with Ludwig. "Guess who I met in our passage?"

"Who?" Ludwig was holding a fizzling test tube over a bunsen burner.

"Paul Protheroe. Prying as usual, I suppose. He said he wanted the downstairs lav, but he didn't go there when I showed it him. How're you doing?"

"Not too good. All this equipment's so damned makeshift; I can't get the stuff to precipitate. I hope to goodness Gran doesn't really go and cut off our allowances. I was counting on mine for some new apparatus."

"I know," she said, "we can't get anywhere with what

we've got. I'd got it all worked out that I wouldn't need any clothes next quarter; we could have blown the lot, blast it. And I got that catalogue I'd sent for this morning. I was scared silly they'd see it at breakfast. Look."

They pored over its pages for a while. "That would about do us," Ludwig said at last. "But how the hell are we going to get it if Gran stops the allowances?"

"Yes," said Leonora, "I'm sick to death of bowing and scraping and waiting for her to dole out the next lot of cash. You know what I think we should do . . ."

Upstairs, their parents were having a very similar conversation. "Pinching and scraping," said Grisel Ffeathers fretfully, "it's all I do from morning to night, and how she expects us to come up with decent Christmas presents for everyone is more than I can see." She was lying on her sofa looking dismally at a long list of names. One or two had ticks, a few others had tentative suggestions against them: 'handkerchiefs' with a query against Josephine's name, 'cigarettes' with another against Joseph's. "Leonora says she and Ludwig want a new precipitator or some word like that, between them," she went on, "but I don't know whether to encourage them in that messy chemistry of theirs or not. You should have smelt Leonora when she came up to change last night; simply disgusting. I told her so."

"Oh, well." Seward lifted a resigned hand to push a greying lock back from his brow, the young musician's gesture oddly pathetic in his worn middle age. "You might as well let them have it. Nothing's going to stop them that I can see. I've given up." It was all too clear that he had.

"That's all very well, but what am I going to use for money? It costs about five pounds," Grisel said.

"I could let you have something towards it," Seward said. "Say three pounds."

"You? I thought you spent your whole allowance on records this quarter – and very inconsiderate too, with Christmas coming up and all; I don't know what would happen to us if I didn't make the sacrifices I do." She paused, and a look Seward knew only too well crossed her face. "Seward, you took that five pounds!"

"I didn't say five, I said three." The attempt at evasion was doomed to failure.

"I don't care what you said; it's the only explanation. Seward, you're crazy; she'll worm it out of you and then where'll we be? God, as if I hadn't had enough of poverty trailing after you on those beastly concert tours and now you go and get us cut off . . ." She burst into dry habitual tears.

"Don't you worry," Seward patted her shoulder absent-mindedly. "Things will be better after Christmas, you just wait and see."

In the room next door Joseph had lost his temper. "Priss can marry the devil, if she wants to," he said. "I don't give a damn, and if you think I'm going to spend my Christmas buttering up that young fool Brian Duguid you've got another guess coming. I've got better things to do with my time."

It was not often that Emily dared cross him when he was in this mood, but this time much was at stake. "But, Joseph dear," she began, "it's such a chance for poor Priss. How's she ever to meet any young men, cooped up the way she is down here? It's so unfair the way your mother lets Mary have a flat in town and keeps poor Priss here to be bullied, you know it is."

53

"Of course it's unfair." He was unusually reasonable. "But I don't know what you expect me to do about it. Nothing I say's going to make Mother change her mind. And I'm not sure I'd bother if it would. Priss is such a little fool she'd get in all kinds of trouble if she had a flat of her own . . . But I wouldn't be surprised if we couldn't set one up for ourselves after Christmas some time."

"What?" Her face lighted up for a minute, then clouded again. "Oh, Joseph, you've not been on the black market again?"

"Black market! Hark at her. The black market's years out of date. Now don't you worry; it's safe as houses, and if it works, you'll have your flat in town yet, and Priss can take her choice of young men. If she can find any that are fools enough, which I doubt."

Mrs Ffeathers had been alone since Paul Protheroe left her. For a while she had sat, her hands folded on her lap, the picture of a well-preserved old lady brooding over a virtuous life. At last she smiled to herself. "Yes," she said, "that should do it; and if one won't the other will." She got up and crossed the room to where her big purple bag lay on the table. She got out a cheque book and a piece of paper and practised signatures for a while until she had one that satisfied her. Then she made out a cheque for fifty pounds to Josephine Ffeathers and signed her name at the bottom, then, with a little smile, she blotted the cheque, turned it over, picked up a different pen, and signed it rather boldly across the back. This done, she got out a doctor's prescription and a little pad of prescription blanks and worked for a while at it. At last she was satisfied; an exquisitely touching smile illuminated her face and she rang the bell. "Ask Miss Smith to come to me immediately after lunch," she said to the maid who answered it.

Four

Patience would never forget that tense week before Christmas. Mrs Ffeathers' five pounds was not returned and under her relentless inquisitorial proddings the household broke more and more into suspicious family units. There was whispering in corridors and hurried conferences broke out in the unsympathetic corners of futuristic rooms.

Patience avoided these, though Mark made various efforts to enrol her in the Brigance brigade, as he called it. "We've nothing to hide; come on, Patience, and hold our hands." The remark was aimed clear across the big, blank drawing room to where Ludwig and Leonora were deep in talk over a catalogue. Ludwig ignored it, but Leonora raised dark eyes to stare coldly across the room at Mark for a minute.

"Lord," he said, "talk about Medusa. Come and cheer us up, Patience, there's a dear; we need it. I'm having fits about the allowances and Mar's scared stiff about what's going to happen to Tony Wetherall. You don't know what surprises Gran's planning for Christmas, do you? I bet she's got some honeys up her sleeve."

"No, I don't." Patience was relieved that it was the truth. "But she looks awfully pleased with herself." Mrs Ffeathers had remained in her room for the last few days, in order, perhaps, to underline the disgrace in which her family lay. Immured there, she held long conferences with Mrs Marshland, the housekeeper, and badgered Patience for information about what went on downstairs. Patience had begun by refusing to tell tales. Mrs Ffeathers had thereupon threatened to cut her out of her will and Patience had urged her to do so. This surprised the old lady, who promptly burst into tears – very decorative ones, as an actress should – and told Patience she was a heartless ingrate. It seemed to Patience that perhaps she was. After all, except for Mark no one but old Mrs Ffeathers had made any particular effort to see that she was happy or even comfortable in this strange household. Why should she deny the old woman the gossip that was obviously life's blood to her?

From then on she doled out innocuous scraps of information with what relish she could give them, hoping that by sharing them out evenly among the family she would do real harm to no one. Joseph and Josephine had quarrelled at the dinner table – the old lady's eyes sparkled; Mark and Mary had gone into Brighton on a mysterious errand – "Mark didn't ask you, eh? You're slipping, Patience." Leonora and Ludwig were more silent than ever and did not even talk about fowl pest at meals. Patience did not add that their mother came down to breakfast every morning with eyes almost closed with crying, while their father was composing a fugue of inconceivable dreariness on the white piano in the drawing room – Mrs Ffeathers had heard that for herself. "Music," she sniffed. "I could do better myself. Used to accompany myself in one show – scarlet boots on the pedals and the gallery in tears. What're the white mice doing – Emily and Priss?"

"Making Christmas presents." Patience was delighted to have so innocuous an answer.

"Ugh. Ink-wipers and pincushions and sweet little flowered bags. And I thought Joseph was a bright boy once. You be careful who you marry, Patience, or see he dies young. I'll always be grateful to my Joseph. A tower of strength while he lasted: never missed a cue or muffed an entrance, and died like a gentleman, just when it suited me best. None of his children can hold a candle to him, nor his grandchildren. You wouldn't have found him dangling around an old lady's apron-strings for her money, so I tell them."

It was the only time Patience ever heard her refer to Mr Ffeathers. Mostly, their conversations consisted of a string of probing questions from Mrs Ffeathers about the behaviour of the other members of the party, which she parried as best she might, though with an uncomfortable feeling that she was wasting her time. What Mrs Ffeathers did not deduce from her silences, she undoubtedly found out from Mrs Marshland, who acted as chief of staff to a lively intelligence service of white-capped maids. Privacy was impossible in that house; many of the doors had glass panes and there were telephones in every room, with Mrs Ffeathers acting as unofficial switchboard operator.

"I never thought hell would be so comfortable," Mark said to Patience on the morning of Christmas Eve. "And you can tell Gran I said that, too." She had surprised herself by confiding to him the difficulty she had in making her reports at once interesting and harmless. "What are you doing this afternoon?" he went on. "Are you on duty? How about a walk? I warn you, dinner tonight will be no joke. Let's go and do a little shouting ahead of time and then maybe we'll be able to behave."

"I wish I could, but I've got some jobs to do for Mrs Ffeathers." It was close enough to the truth, Patience thought crossly as she let herself quietly out of a side door half an hour later and started off across the downs towards Leyning.

It was a ridiculous enough expedition, she thought to herself; three miles there and three back to buy chocolate animals for the whole party. "For their stockings," Mrs Ffeathers had explained. "I do like an old-fashioned Christmas with stockings along the mantelshelf." She was a parody of a stage dear old lady. "And they must be a surprise, so don't tell a soul where you're going. Slip out the back way; no one'll notice; they're all dead to the world in the afternoon."

It was all very well, thought Patience, but a little company would have shortened the walk; besides, if she had asked Mark, he would have driven her over in no time. But Mrs Ffeathers had been insistent to the point of a thinly veiled allusion to Patience's four pounds a week and it had seemed simpler to give in and promise. After all, thought Patience, she should have an answer from college soon after Christmas, and she had already made up her mind that even if they could not help her, she would make that an excuse to leave Featherstone Hall. By then she would have saved enough money for that impossible fare up to Suffolk and could go and take council with her friends, the Cunninghams. Two more weeks at the outside, she said to herself as she started down the long slope to Leyning, and anything for a quiet life in the meantime.

She found the shop that specialised in chocolate animals easily enough and gave them her order, thinking how characteristic it was of old Mrs Ffeathers to take it for granted she would use her own sweet coupons. Then she went to a chemist with the prescription Mrs Ffeathers had given her. "I can never sleep at Christmas time; it's all much too exciting." By this time Mrs Ffeathers had been the frail old invalid.

That left her with the last errand, the one she had been half-consciously putting off. Mrs Ffeathers had called her back at the last minute. "Just cash me this cheque at the Black Stag, would you? They know me there, and I don't want to run out of petty cash over Christmas."

Fifty pounds was a lot of petty cash, Patience thought, turning reluctant steps towards the Black Stag. She always felt uncomfortable cashing cheques anywhere but at the right bank; it seemed – ridiculously, she knew – as if you were asking a favour. But when Mrs Ffeathers produced the cheque she had already lost her struggle over the secrecy of the expedition and did not want to start the business of veiled threat and honeyed cajolement all over again. She had simply taken it and accepted the old lady's assurance that she had dealt with the Black Stag ever since she moved to the Hall. "And with Joseph in the house that's plenty of dealing," she had concluded.

Just the same, Patience felt acutely uncomfortable as she waited in the antler-hung hallway of the inn while the elegant young lady who condescended to act as barmaid retired with the cheque to the nether regions. When she returned she was more haughty than ever. "No; sorry," she said, "we don't cash cheques for transients."

Patience felt herself blushing. "But Mrs Ffeathers is not a transient. She says she's been dealing here for years."

"That's as may be," said the young lady, "but Mr Pangbourne says we don't cash her cheques. I'm sorry to inconvenience you, I'm sure" – she was clearly delighted – "but that's what he said. You can see him if you want to."

This finally routed Patience. "Oh, no, thank you; I'll just have to tell Mrs Ffeathers . . ." The young lady had turned her back and Patience dwindled unhappily down the hall and out into the street.

Not a successful expedition. She had paid for the chocolate animals and Mrs Ffeathers' pills out of her own dwindling resources, and would have to give up her project of a relaxed and Featherstoneless tea in The Old Bunhouse, across the road; and anyway, it was getting dark.

It was quite dark when she got back to Featherstone Hall, and Mrs Ffeathers was full of solicitude.

"Inconsiderate old party that I am," she greeted Patience, with eyes even more sparkling than usual, "I was so set on my sweets I clean forgot how soon the afternoons close in these days. But you're such a capable girl; I'm sure you can find your way anywhere in the dark." She seemed to find something particularly amusing in the idea. "And did you manage without anyone knowing? What a clever girl!"

She was being mocked, Patience thought, and wondered just why. It added, somehow, to an uncomfortable feeling that had been in the back of her mind all afternoon. There was more, she could not help thinking, to this expedition than Mrs Ffeathers had let on.

"Here are your pills." She took the little packet out of

her bag. "But I'm afraid I couldn't cash the cheque. They didn't seem to know you at the Black Stag."

Mrs Ffeathers burst into delighted laughter. "I don't suppose they did. I've never bought so much as a bottle of soda water there. Oh, Patience, you are a gullible pet; it's really too bad to take advantage of you. I really half thought they'd cash it for you, you're so blessedly sure of yourself. That's why I made it for fifty, just to be sure." She took the cheque from Patience, tore it in tiny pieces and put it carefully in the centre of the fire.

"But I don't understand," said Patience, half puzzled, half angry.

"I don't suppose you do. That cheque, my love, was one I stopped at the bank yesterday. I told them someone had taken it out of my book and I couldn't be answerable for what happened to it. And if the bank ever shows whoever looked at it at the Black Stag my signature – and if *they've* any kind of a memory, which I don't suppose they have – they'll say the signatures were bad forgeries. Just the kind of thing a girl who didn't know me very well might try to do. *Now* d'you understand?" Mrs Ffeathers sat back in her chair, her bright eyes sparkling with satisfaction. "*Now* I think you'll tell me what they say about me in the dining room, my girl, and any other little thing I want to know, and without quite so many of your holier-than-thou airs and graces either, or you may find yourself answering some awkward questions from the police."

"But you wouldn't . . ." Patience's voice shook.

"Oh, wouldn't I? You ask the others; they know. But don't you worry." She leaned forward and patted Patience's hand as it lay limply on the arm of her chair. "I won't do it. I like you, Patience; you've got a will of your own and I respect you for it. Don't forget; I've left you all my money, and I mean it. Just you be reasonable with me, and I'll be fair with you, but I want you to know you've got to treat me with respect. I've lived for ninety years and always had my way, and I'm not going to be crossed now. I just wanted to make you see that. And now you run away and change your dress. Priss's and Mary's young men are both going to be here for dinner, and you want to look your best for them – not to mention Mark." She gleamed up at Patience from under exquisitely plucked eyebrows. "And mind you, not a word about this afternoon's jaunt or I'll have the police on you." She laughed as she spoke, but the words still rang uncomfortably in Patience's head as she changed into one of her two evening dresses. How far was Mrs Ffeathers serious? Surely not at all? But she found it hard to convince herself of this. Suddenly, overwhelmingly, she longed to leave Featherstone Hall that night. No matter where she went, so long as it was away.

There was a light tap on her door. "And remember" – Mrs Ffeathers was resplendent in black velvet – "if you run away, I'll call the police the minute you're out of the house."

Afterwards, Patience wondered why she had not left the house on the spot, but at the time it seemed, for some reason, cowardly. She grinned at old Mrs Ffeathers. "I'm not running away," she said. "Why should I?"

The long glass table in the white dining room was decorated with holly and red ribbon bows. It did not, Patience thought, make the room any less blankly funereal. It merely looked as if someone had decided to send red flowers to a corpse. She said so to Mark, who sat next to her.

"Yes," he said. "Karl Marx, no doubt. I don't know what induced Gran to let Mother and Uncle Joseph loose on this house. It was quite inhabitable before they laid on all the chromium. Another of her experiments, I suppose. Which reminds me; where on earth did you disappear to this afternoon? I looked all over for you; Mar and I went into Brighton to sit on Father Christmas's knee. I even bearded the lion in her den and asked Gran where you were, and she cackled just like the witch in the gingerbread house and said, 'Wouldn't you like to know?'. I was really afraid she'd turned you into a white mouse or something. Not that she could," he hastened to add. "A white deer, perhaps, but never a mouse."

Patience laughed, relieved that he had talked himself away from the question of where she had been. She was not sure she wanted to talk about that. She looked up the long table, searching for a new subject. "Full house tonight." Hardly brilliant, but it would do.

"Yes, Christmas Eve in the workhouse, and the paupers lined up with their basins and spoons." There was a bitter note in Mark's voice than she did not like to hear. "What do you think of our young men on approval?" he went on, glancing at the other side of the table, where Mary was voluble beside her Tony, and Priss silent misery beside Brian Duguid.

"Priss doesn't seem to think much of hers."

"No, I'm afraid Aunt Emily's missed the bus this time – not that she doesn't always, poor old duck. And Gran's revelling in it; just look at her. She's having such a good time she's forgotten all about shocking Tony Wetherall. It's her favourite indoor sport, you know, frightening poor Mary's young men away. Give me a hand turning her off if she tries it after dinner, will you? I don't think much of him myself, but Mar seems to want him and I suppose she knows best."

"I suppose so," Patience agreed, casting a doubtful glance at Tony's amiable if unimpressive countenance. He had turned for the moment to Priss, who sat on his other side, and was making weekend conversation about the weather.

"All things to all men," breathed Mark in her ear. "Don't forget he's in public relations, God help him."

"At least it's a job." Patience felt suddenly moved to defend the innocuous Tony.

"Spoke the career girl. Don't tell me you think a job would add to my natural charm. I never found anything I wanted to work at, myself."

"You did at Cambridge."

"Don't tell me Mother has been boasting about my honours and glories. I didn't think she was that human a parent. But work at Cambridge wasn't work, my good girl, not within the meaning of the act. Nobody paid me for it, for one thing; quite the reverse."

"And being paid puts you off? It's an unusual point of view."

"All my points of view are unusual. I specialise in them. But, Patience, would you really prefer me as a working man? Because if so I shall have to take it seriously under consideration. What would you prefer? A bowler and a briefcase in Whitehall or a topper and an umbrella in the City?"

"Oh, the top hat by all means; it would suit you." Patience made a quick grab at the lighter side of the question. It was, she felt, showing dangerous signs of getting out of hand. After all, what affair was Mark's career of hers?

"Come now, don't wash your hands of me." He shared his grandmother's disconcerting gift for mind-reading. "I was beginning to hope—"

His hopes were interrupted by his grandmother's powerful voice. "When you've quite finished, Mark, perhaps you'll be so good as to open the door for me." While they had been absorbed in their suddenly meaningful conversation she had risen and drawn her black velvet – and the other ladies – around her, so that they were now grouped behind Mark and Patience. He hurried to obey her, only muttering under his breath to Patience as he went: "Look out; the old girl's getting jealous." Of whom, Patience was still wondering as she poured the coffee for the other ladies in the drawing room.

The men were allowed no extension of their usual ten minutes' grace in the dining room, nor, Patience suspected, would they have been particularly grateful for one. They were an ill-assorted lot, she thought, watching Joseph stalk into the room ahead of a silent group. Tony Wetherall, she noticed with amusement, had managed to find a subject in common with Brian Duguid – or did their animated conversation about the clubs they did and did not belong to merely conceal their discomfort at the odd Christmas Eve they found themselves sharing?

She looked around the room. What, after all, was so odd about it? A handsome and prosperous-looking family gathered in the matriarch's house for Christmas. What could be more right and proper? And of course the occasion made for a certain extra feeling of formality; it was ridiculous to imagine that there was anything more in the air than that. Yet she could not help it. The scene was a caricature of a family party.

Mrs Ffeathers had risen and was dominating the room in her black velvet. "Lady Macbeth tonight," whispered Mark in Patience's ear.

"Well," said the old lady in her surprisingly beautiful voice, "here we are all together for another family Christmas and I think we should celebrate it by doing something sociable – playing games, perhaps. Not happy families, I think" – a wicked, bright eye swept the room – "but something a little more exciting. Hunt the fiver would be fun, don't you think, Seward? And blind man's buff, with me for blind man. But to begin with, I think perhaps some charades would be nice; I'll pick one side and Patience can pick the other. No buts, Patience; it's time you learnt to take your place properly. After all, any day now you may be running this house yourself."

Effectively silenced, Patience dutifully picked her side, grateful for the support Mark was soon giving her. She hated amateur theatricals of any kind and it was thin consolation to notice that so did everyone else in the room – with the obvious exception of Mrs Ffeathers, who was, after all, a professional, and the possible one of Brian Duguid who was throwing himself with evangelical enthusiasm into the problem of choosing a word for Patience's team. She found herself wondering whether some of his joyful energy was not due to the fact that Priss was drooping lethargically on the other side. "Poor Priss," muttered Mark as he swathed

67

Patience in yards of black muslin, "they'd better cast her as a domino with all those white buttons."

Patience laughed. "Don't be mean. It was a good idea putting them on that black dress; Mary says they're madly fashionable this year."

"And Mary should know." He glanced approvingly at his sister in her sideswept crimson. "Careless of you not to pick Tony, Patience; just look at him suffering over there, poor man. Gran's telling him she accompanied herself on the piano in red boots; I can tell by the gleam in her eye. And it may have been a good idea" – he reverted to Priss's dress – "but you must admit the execution is lamentable. Poor Priss has never done anything right in her life."

"Mark, you are a cat; I don't know why they say women are worse than men." It was time to change the subject; he was going to start protesting something or other. "How on earth are we going to act 'of'?"

"Suggestion, of course. You be the Queen of Sheba and I'm your devoted slave. Or if you prefer it I'll be 'Of Street' and you can walk over me. I'd enjoy that."

"Oh, you're impossible." But she was laughing as she turned to Brian Duguid who had some extremely practical suggestions as to how they should act out 'inoffensiveness': "We did it when I was in boy scout camp once, I remember, and it was the greatest success. I was a riot as the Loch Ness monster, though I do say so."

"That's it," Mark joined in, "and this time you can come on in your boy scout uniform at the end and that'll be 'inoffensiveness'. Come on, Patience, you're on as the barmaid. Your dress is just lerrvely; you should always wear black."

The evening did nothing to shake Patience's dislike of amateur dramatics. She got through her part in their own charade as best she might and was relieved when it was instantly guessed by Joseph who had, she suspected, had a rendezvous with Mark at the dining room sideboard. "Told you we wouldn't be left struggling for long," Mark said, helping her out of the white sheet in which she had impersonated inoffensiveness. "Now for the front row of the stalls. I warn you Gran's terrific, but it's as well to watch her."

In fact, Patience found herself liking old Mrs Ffeathers better than ever before as she watched her act out 'antidisestablishmentarianism' *à la* Ruth Draper with only the most negligible support from the rest of her team who were only too glad to bask in her shadow. She was so patently disappointed when Brian Duguid tactlessly guessed the word at the fifth syllable that Patience found herself insisting, as rival captain, that she go ahead and act out the rest. "Bright idea," muttered Mary from the sofa where Tony Wetherall had somehow managed to join her. "Perhaps even Gran'll be satisfied by that and we can get on to the next stage of the ordeal."

"What's that?" Tony's pink face looked nervous. It was not, Patience could see, at all what he had expected of a country Christmas.

"Christmas stockings, my pet; all along the mantelpiece in Gran's room." Mary had obviously decided to carry off the situation with a high hand, and Patience could not help admiring her for it. And after all, what situation was there? There was nothing so odd about charades on Christmas Eve. She looked round the room as she had done earlier in the evening, trying to decide what it was that gave the occasion its peculiarly explosive quality. Surely not old Mrs

Ffeathers, gleefully clowning her way through her act? What could be more sympathetic than the old stager enjoying a last fling on the boards?

At the same time you could not really blame her family, some looking uncomfortable, some bored. It must have happened to them so many times before. But there was more to it than that. The conversation that Seward and his wife had been carrying on at intervals throughout the evening had an unmistakable note of urgency. She was pressing him to some course of action with a vigour Patience had hardly thought her capable of. It was surprising, she thought, that none of the others seemed to have noticed it, but then they all had their own preoccupations. Mary had been busy all evening trying to make the scene as normal as possible for Tony's benefit – a full-time job with her grandmother letting off fireworks at more than the usual rate. Joseph had spent every minute he had been able to in the dining room and looked scarcely the better for it; any minute now, Patience thought, he would start pinching somebody. His wife had spent the evening following her daughter with large, anxious eyes, putting in a word here and a nervous twist to the offending rows of buttons there, and receiving in return, Patience could see, considerably less than courtesy. Priss was in one of the cold black moods Patience remembered from their childhood and had so comprehensively snubbed Brian Duguid that even his lamblike spirit was roused to retaliation. This took the form of a devoted attention to Patience that Mark found extremely trying.

"Can't you get rid of your boyfriend?" he muttered under cover of the round of semi-spontaneous clapping that greeted Mrs Ffeathers' exit. "I want to talk to you."

"Now?" Patience was not sure she was ready for conversation on the level his tone implied.

"No time like the present. On the first day of Christmas . . ." But the clapping had died suddenly and Brian Duguid heard and took him up. "Oh, good egg; let's sing some carols. Christmas isn't Christmas without them, is it, Patience?"

Patience was spared the trouble of replying by the reappearance of Mrs Ffeathers who ordered them all upstairs to her own room. "A little Christmas surprise." Her caricature of a dear old lady was perfectly in tune with the occasion.

Five

Trimmed with holly, old Mrs Ffeathers' red plush room was more than ever the saloon bar. An appropriate fire blazed in the hearth, and beside it, under a bush of mistletoe, Mrs Ffeathers sat enthroned in her great, red chair. She watched her family sardonically as they shuffled in and found their seats, the younger members of the party uncomfortable on cushions round the fire, their elders in the ring of chairs behind them.

"I see you can all resist the temptation to kiss me." Mrs Ffeathers cast a half humorous eye upwards.

"We didn't dare, Mama; you looked so regal." Joseph stooped from his favourite position on the hearth to rectify the omission.

Mark had settled on the floor beside Patience. "Lord," he whispered, reaching over to touch one of the row of socks and stockings laid out like limp corpses along the hearth, "I'd forgotten about the stockings. I wonder what the old dear found when she was routing about for mine."

"Does she get them herself?"

"You bet she does . . . too good a chance to miss. Worried about your guilty secrets? You'd better be; she'll be on to them . . ."

"Mark, I'm in awful trouble." Patience paused. It sounded such an absurd story.

"What's the matter? I thought there was something odd about the way you vanished this afternoon. Come on," he saw her hesitation, "tell your Uncle Mark. Free advice, total secrecy, no unnecessary questions asked."

"It seems so silly," she began, but as she did so, the buzz of conversation that had covered them died away. Mrs Ffeathers was in command again.

"Now" – a piercing eye travelled around the room – "before we fill the stockings, I promised you a little surprise. I hope you noticed" – again that penetrating glance – "that I didn't say a pleasant little surprise. I wouldn't like you to think that I'd got you up here on false pretences. But one of you must have a pretty good idea what I'm talking about." She allowed her pause to stretch out into an uneasy silence.

"Damn, damn, damn," muttered Mark in Patience's ear. "It's that blasted five pounds. Poor old Mary; it'll finish Tony Wetherall once and for all. Can't you create a diversion, Patience? She might take it from you."

"Not her." Patience spoke with such feeling that he turned enquiring eyes.

"So that's the trouble? Shown her claws already, has she? You must tell me all about it afterwards."

But Mrs Ffeathers was satisfied with the unhappy rustle she had stirred in the room. "Yes," she went on, "not a very pleasant surprise for one of you, I'm afraid. But what a pity to spoil the festive season for the others." She mocked Christmas cheer. "Perhaps we should have our fun first, and keep business to the last. I hope you've all brought

73

your presents with you." She turned, totally charming now, to Tony Wetherall, who was sitting, blank-faced, beside Mary. "I hope we don't bore you with our old-fashioned customs. I do like a real Christmas, with stockings along the mantelshelf; I expect my granddaughter warned you."

"Yes, she did say something about it." Tony's self-possession, usually so iron-clad, had totally deserted him and he spoke through an outgrown stammer. "I brought a few little things . . . I hope it was all right . . ."

Mary had seen a chance. "Gran," – she could be very engaging when she chose – "isn't the surprise a bit of a family affair? Do you think Tony and Brian want to be bothered with it?"

"I don't suppose they do." The old lady allowed herself a sybilline chuckle. "But I thought they were here just because they were family – or almost." A meaning look from Mary's ringless left hand to Priss's. "No, no; they're the guests in my house" – a powerful emphasis on the 'my' – "and they're entitled to know what goes on in it. Now, out with the presents; there are paper and ribbon on the centre table if anyone hasn't wrapped theirs. Patience, where's the parcel you got for me? And, oh," – as Patience handed it to her – "get me my Bovril, will you? I'll have it while we're filling the stockings. And two pills tonight." She raised her voice as Patience reached the door that led into her bathroom. "I'm not going to miss my sleep for anyone."

Glad to be alone for a minute, Patience half shut the bathroom door and turned up the tiny flame under the pan holding Mrs Ffeathers' evening Bovril and milk. The dark brown brew began to bubble at the edges almost at once and she turned quickly to the cupboard for the bottle of sleeping pills. Mrs Ffeathers hated to have her milk boiled. She shook two tablets from the almost empty bottle and noticed as she did so that the new bottle she had put beside it earlier in the evening was no longer on the shelf. Could Mrs Ffeathers have moved it to the bedside table? She knew that the doctor disapproved of this habit, and warned herself to investigate later in the evening.

The pills were totally dissolved by now, and she returned to the other room where the stocking filling was well under way in an atmosphere of more gaiety than she would have believed possible.

"Good." Mrs Ffeathers reached out a slightly trembling hand for the cup. "That ought to put hair on my chest." A wicked eye surveyed the company for reactions. "Now, Joseph, the brandy, and no nonsense with it on the way."

Silently, Joseph moved from his chair by the fire to the corner cupboard and brought back a half full brandy bottle.

"A good slug, mind," said his mother. "What you'd give yourself – if you could get it."

Obediently, he poured a full measure into the steaming cup and returned the bottle to its cupboard. She sipped. "Ah, nice and strong. Now, where are we? The stockings all filled? Just about time for my surprise, then."

"But aren't we going to open them first?" The interruption came, surprisingly, from silent Seward.

"Why? Can't you wait to play with your new toys till the morning? Or have you some other reason?"

He shrank. "No, no; I just thought . . . We always used to open them on Christmas Eve."

"Do let's, Gran." Mark spoke up from beside Patience. "What's the use of waiting till tomorrow morning?"

"Oh, very well." Her tone was surprisingly subdued. "Have it your own way. Open them up quickly, though; and let me have a little peace. I'm tired of the whole pack of you."

The present-opening was a masterpiece of delaying action. By the time the last piece of tissue paper had been carefully refolded and the last shred of ribbon picked up off the carpet, it was after midnight and Mrs Ffeathers was drooping in her chair. "What d'you think," Mark whispered to Patience, "a reprieve?"

"Might be." Patience looked round the room, wondering who would have the skill, not to mention the courage, to persuade the old lady to go to bed without dropping her bomb. Certainly not Priss, drooping at the little table with the unwelcome teapot. Brian Duguid was hovering behind her, gloomily aware that this was where he was expected to be, and making the best of it by passing cups of tea and staying away for as long as possible. He had just handed a cup to Joseph, who scowled as he accepted it. No hope of Joseph's influence with his mother. And Josephine, who sat on the sofa near him, would be no more use. Patience's eye travelled along the seated circle: no hope from Emily, who sat absorbed in some hypochondriac trance, and certainly none from Seward and his wife who were remote from the room, engaged in a furious quarrel in dumb show and whispers.

The last cup of tea had been passed by now and Mrs Ffeathers seemed to be making a great effort to rouse herself. Patience turned, more desperately, to the circle of young people on the floor. Mark was no use, though she paused, regretfully, at the too handsome profile; nor yet

Leonora and Ludwig who sat on the floor on the other side of her, distanced from the party, as usual, in some discussion of their own. Beyond them, completing the circle on the floor, were Mary and Tony Wetherall, head to head. It was a chance. Deliberately, she turned to Mrs Ffeathers. "It looks as if Mary's got a real present," she said.

Mrs Ffeathers started upright in her chair. "Well, Mary, are we to congratulate you – again?"

Mary blushed, becomingly of course, and turned to Tony. "I don't know," she began, but he interrupted her.

"I hope you're going to congratulate *me*, Mrs Ffeathers. If you'll only persuade Mary that we don't need to wait for anything to get engaged. She wants to wait until after your 'surprise'," he explained.

"She's a very clever girl," said her grandmother. "All right, Mary, your point. I'm sleepy tonight and I can't be bothered with you all for another minute. My surprise will keep – don't you worry about that." The bright, malevolent eyes travelled round the room. "Now be off with you, for goodness' sake. No; I won't be kissed tonight." She waved Josephine away. "I've had enough kissing for one lifetime, and if you haven't, it's just too bad."

After that, there was no ceremony in their flight. Only Patience lingered for a minute in the doorway. "Are you sure you wouldn't like me to stay and help you to bed? You must be dreadfully tired."

"I am dreadfully tired." The beautiful voice shook and spoiled the mimicry. "But not so tired I'm going to have a child like you fussing over undressing me. I may be ninety-one, but I'm not incapable yet, and when I am, I hope to God I'm dead. Get along with you now; Mark

77

is waiting for you outside. But remember what I told you about him."

"Good-night, then." Patience closed the door gently behind her and found Mark shaking with silent laughter. "There's not much gets past our Gran," he said. "What did she tell you about me, Patience?"

"Oh, nothing, really." The blush was uncontrollable.

"Bad as that, was it? Let's for the Lord's sake go get ourselves a drink and you can tell me all about it." Taking her elbow, he steered her towards his room. "Come on, I landed a bottle of Scotch in Leyning this afternoon. Mary and Tony'll be at it already, if I know her."

But when they got there, the room was dark. Patience hung back but Mark urged her forward.

"Come on, Mrs Grundy; to hell with the neighbours, you need a drink. Mar and Tony'll be here any minute to have their health drunk. She deserves it, too, landing him under Gran's nose like that."

"Do you think her 'surprise' is about the five pounds she lost?"

"Sure it is. I expect she's found out who took it. Or maybe she thinks she has and wants to frighten them into admitting it. Here, this'll fix you up." He handed her the tall, warm glass of bedroom Scotch and soda.

"Thank you." A sound in the hall made her look hopefully round, expecting Mary, but nobody came. "I really ought to go." She made to rise as he sat down beside her on the cushioned divan.

"Please don't." He put a hand on her shoulder and something fizzed inside her. "I want to talk to you. I've been wanting to all day." He was overwhelmingly close to her now, as he took her glass away and put it beside his on the bedside table. "Tell me it's happened to you too, Patience. It can't just be me, surely? Tell me it's hit you too."

"What, Mark—?" What was happening to her? Panic hit her. She was losing control.

"Don't say 'This is so sudden'," he interrupted her. "I couldn't bear it. I'm asking you to marry me, Patience. I love you. It's the strangest thing. I never thought it would happen to me. I had quite different plans. Please listen to me. I'm not much of a prospect as I stand, I know, but say yes and I'll turn to and work like a Trojan. You'll be the making of me. You're what I needed; someone to work for, bowler hat and all."

"But it *is* sudden." She moved a little away, afraid of what would happen if he touched her again. Something in her was out of hand, and it scared her. "We hardly know each other, Mark. And everything here is so strange. I don't like the feel of things. It's not the time."

"But that's just what it is, you know. It's our moment. Let's take it, Patience. This is a hell of a household, but we could cope with it together."

His hand was on her shoulder again, trying to turn her to face him, and panic suddenly won. She broke free and stood up. "Not tonight, Mark. Not after all that's gone on. It's too quick, not right, I can't—"

"Then I'll ask you again in the morning. Think it over, dear, darling Patience, and I'll ask again in the morning."

She was shaking all over as she fled to her room, but there was a warm glow inside her. He would ask again in the morning. She must think it over. She must sleep on it, this new feeling that did such strange things to her. She had been alone for so long. Was this the end of it?

Getting into bed, she remembered that she had never checked on Mrs Ffeathers' pills. Too late now. Wild horses would not get her back into that room. Mrs Ffeathers was dangerous, her threats not to be dismissed. She should have told Mark about it, but how could she? Maybe she would in the morning. She fell asleep, thinking of the morning, smiling to herself.

The morning came too soon. Sitting up, dazed, in bed, she heard again the sound that had awoken her, a scream from the room next door. Her dressing gown was inside out, one slipper had vanished, but somehow, still half asleep, she was at the door leading to Mrs Ffeathers' room. Opening it, she stood appalled. Andrews, the elegant parlour maid, was having hysterics over a dropped breakfast tray, coffee and hot milk soaking silently into the deep red carpet. One crimson-nailed hand held back the heavy red velvet curtains of the four-poster bed; but the bed was empty. It was beyond it, at the big wing-chair, that the maid directed her screams. Hurrying round to the fireplace, Patience saw why. Mrs Ffeathers was still sitting as she had when they left her the night before, sitting still, too still . . .

The maid screamed again and Josephine appeared in the other doorway. "What on earth's the matter?" Then, "My God . . . Mother!" She pulled her ostrich-feather wrap more closely around her and stood for a minute, taking it in. Then she turned. "For God's sake, Andrews, pull yourself together and pick up that china. We shall have to phone the doctor.

Patience, could you, while I dress?" Executive again, she turned and left the room.

Patience paused for a moment and watched Andrews tearfully picking up broken china. "You'd better stay," she said, "till I get back."

Andrews looked up at her, sniffling. "Oh, miss, I can't. Not alone, so help me I can't."

"What's the trouble?" Relieved, Patience turned to see Joseph in the doorway. "Mother ill?"

Incoherently, and crying now herself, she began to explain, but a glance at the figure in the chair told him enough. "Right," he said, "I'll handle it. You and Andrews stay here till I get back, will you?" He closed the door softly behind him and they heard the key turn in the lock.

Andrews instantly went off into hysterics again and Patience had her hands full for the next few minutes. As she alternately bullied and cajoled the sobbing girl into comparative calmness she wondered, half-consciously, why Joseph had wanted them both to stay. Just as well, perhaps. "Come on," she said, "help me to clear this up."

However, Andrews was making the most of her license to hysteria. Better to get her under control before the doctor came. Patience hurried to Mrs Ffeathers' bathroom for her bottle of smelling salts. But the small bottle was not in its place and though she looked hastily among Mrs Ffeathers' collection of pills, lotions and creams she could see no sign of it. Could she have left it in her own room? But when she tried her door she found that it was locked too. She and Andrews were shut in with the body. She shivered and Andrews went off into a new tornado of sobs. "Here—" Patience hurried to the cupboard and brought out

81

Mrs Ffeathers' brandy bottle – "drink this." She poured a generous measure into the glass from beside the bed and made Andrews swallow it.

Joseph opened the door. "Sorry to leave you like that; I didn't want the whole family in here. Dr Findlayson and the police will be here right away."

"The police?" Patience asked.

"Findlayson said I'd better call them as it was so sudden. Of course there's nothing in it – but you know it's odd just the same. She was a tough old girl." They were the most affectionate words Patience had ever heard him speak of his mother. "You were the last to leave her last night, weren't you?" Was there a new note of calculation in his voice?

"Yes, I thought she might need help. She seemed so dreadfully tired."

"Yes, of course." He was thinking of something else. "No need for you two to stay now. Patience, you look all in. Why don't you go and lie down for a bit before the police get here?"

He wanted to be rid of her, and why not? Besides, she was still in her dressing gown. "Thank you; I believe I will."

She heard him relock the communicating door behind her as she climbed into bed and pulled cold sheets up around her chin. But it was impossible to get warm. She lay there shivering under the pile of blankets for half an hour, then gave it up and got out of bed. Best to get dressed anyway; it was nine o'clock. She had no day-time black to wear, but what did it matter? Mrs Ffeathers had always ridiculed the idea of mourning. 'Of course if it happens to suit you that's something else again,' Patience remembered her saying. Choking back sudden tears, she pulled a wine-coloured dress off its hanger and put it on.

When she opened her door, the house struck her over-wrought senses as strangely silent. There were none of the usual morning noises, no splashings from the bathroom down the hall, no bursts of unmelodious song from Mark's room. Where was everyone? Could no one else have heard Andrews' screams? But Joseph and Josephine must be about somewhere, and besides, even today breakfast must presumably get itself eaten. She hurried downstairs, suddenly sick with loneliness, wanting Mark.

In the dining room, the long table stood laid for fourteen, its decoration of holly and red ribbon still more incongruous in the cold morning light. The small flame hissed under the coffee urn and the hatch to the kitchen stood invitingly open, letting a hint of bacon into the air, but there was nobody there. Patience hesitated in the doorway for a moment, then the sound of excited voices from the kitchen made her turn, almost in flight. On an impulse, she ran upstairs and knocked on Mark's door, but there was no answer. She knocked again, more loudly, then gave it up. She knew, without reasoning, that all the bedrooms were empty. She knocked at Mary's. Silence. At Josephine's. Nothing.

A door at the far end of the hall opened and Brian Duguid's pink face peered short-sightedly out. "I say, have I overslept frightfully?" He looked defenceless in his dressing gown.

"No, no. It's quite early." She could not bring herself to tell him. "No one's started breakfast." She retreated down the stairs, half heard him say, "I thought I heard someone calling," but was too far away to answer.

83

The big drawing room stood empty and unwelcoming in the grey light. Beyond it, the library still had its heavy curtains drawn. No doubt this was one of the hysterical Andrews' duties. Automatically, Patience pulled back the curtains and started at the sudden rattle of their heavy rings in the too silent house. Pausing, as she always did, to look at the rising sweep of the downs outside, she saw two cars speeding along the narrow road from the village. The police already? She hurried to pull the curtains at the next window, where she would get a better view, but as she did so the door at the far end of the room opened and Josephine appeared.

"Good, there you are, Patience. I was just coming to look for you."

Looking past her, Patience saw the family gathered in the little, disused study: Joseph, dominant at the mantelpiece, Seward drooping beside him, their wives huddled on an old sofa, Leonora and Ludwig in a corner as usual, Priss close to them, pleating and unpleating the hem of her dress, Mark and Mary side by side on the window seat. All the Ffeatherses were there and as they turned and slowly, silently gazed at her, she had an overwhelming feeling, worse than any she had suffered as a child, that they were strangers, aliens, the enemy. It was absurd, of course, and half-consciously she turned to Mark for reassurance, but it seemed, strangely, that he did not see her. His back was to the light, so that she could only make out the outline of that handsome face, and he seemed to be looking straight through her.

Pure nerves. She must pull herself together and listen to Joseph. "A sort of family council," he was saying. "Didn't like to disturb you as you were resting, but I'm glad you turned up when you did. You see, there's bound to be a bit of unpleasantness about this – poor old Mother going off so suddenly, you know – and of course we want to draw it as mild as we can. No sense going into anything that'd make the poor old dear look ridiculous – like that idea of hers that someone had stolen five pounds from her. We all know what she was like, but tell a thing like that to the police and there's no knowing what ideas they may not get into their heads. You know what I'm getting at, Patience; least said, soonest mended and all that kind of thing. No reason to expect there'll be any trouble, but the less we all talk, the less trouble there'll be. You see my point?"

"Yes, of course. I won't say anything." If he was protesting too much, she found it impossible to sound convincing at all. And yet it was all perfectly reasonable. So why this feeling of nightmare? Again her eyes sought Mark's, but he had turned to look out of the window behind him.

"Here are the police," he announced flatly. And still he did not meet her eyes.

Six

High up under the roofs of New Scotland Yard, Detective Sergeant Geoffrey Crankshaw and his office mate were reading reports of action taken in country districts. They were supposed to be filing and cross-indexing these for further reference, but in fact they were drinking cups of tea and grumbling.

"I wish I was back on my beat in Bermondsey," said the office mate, demolishing an overblown doughnut. "At least things happened there, even if it was only drunks. Here it's just read, read, read till your eyes fall out of your head. I don't know about you, Crankshaw, but much more of this red tape and sealing wax and I'm packing it in."

"I couldn't agree with you more," said Crankshaw. "I didn't join the force to be turned into a paper pusher. Some of my university friends are earning real money by now, and just look at us! Can't even afford to take a girl out decently."

"Rotten," agreed his office mate. "Still, at least that was a short one." A careful young man, he wiped the sugar off his fingers before dropping a report into the basket marked 'File'.

"Anything interesting?"

"Not particularly. Bit of snappy work by the boys in Sussex. Old lady found dead Christmas morning. First view, natural causes. Poor old lady; excitement of Christmas, sorrowing relatives, the old story. Then the doctor takes a look at her, and she's chock full of sleeping pills."

"Her own?"

"Lord, yes, her own all right, but too damn many of them. The poor old girl went off in her chair and never woke up no more."

"And what did our Sussex friends do about that?"

"Asked twenty-five pages of questions – " he flipped through them rapidly – "and discovered one good reason why the family were sorrowing so. The old thing had cut them off without a bean."

"Too bad. And too bad for us, too." Crankshaw always thought professionally. "Not much motive in that."

"Not much for the family; no. But a whopping great one for the girl she left it all to."

"Not a cat and dog home?"

"No; she'd got beyond that. Apparently she'd left it to just about everything in her time, but last week she sat down and willed it all to a long-lost great-niece – and that was the end of her, poor old thing."

"The great-niece did it? It seems almost too simple."

"I know. To judge by the questions, they could hardly believe their luck. But there it was: motive as big as a barn door; the girl in financial straits; a forged prescription for the sleeping pills; a whole bottle of them among her nylons; the best opportunity of the lot; her fingerprints over everything – the defence'll plead insanity of course, but I doubt if they'll get away with it – and goodbye Patience Smith."

87

"What?" Crankshaw knocked over the table between the two desks and snatched the report. Five minutes later, white in the face and quite unaware of the black ink smudge across his left cheek, he was stuttering slightly at his superior officer who, knowing him for a calm young man, listened with unusual patience.

"You see, sir," said Crankshaw for the fourth time, "I know her. I swear she didn't do it. Couldn't have."

The tall, grey-haired man behind the executive's desk looked worried. "I understand how you feel, Crankshaw, but it's a strong case – a very strong case. I don't quite see how we could interfere. There's been no question of their asking our help. And it isn't even as if we had any facts to contribute. Of course," he went on kindly, "*I* know you well enough to take this feeling of yours seriously – you're not usually wrong about people – but you can hardly expect them to do so at Leyning."

He was being almost impossibly kind, Crankshaw knew. He flogged an unresponsive brain; there must be some fact to prove his point if he could only come far enough out of his shock to think coherently. His thoughts dived down improbable corridors – Patience saying goodbye in Suffolk, her help on his case there – all ancient history, all useless. Then he almost ground his teeth at his own stupidity. "I've got it, sir."

"Yes?"

"You remember you sent me along to look out for that shoplifter at Gogarty's? Well, an odd thing happened there the first day I was on duty. I ran into this Patience Smith, or rather, to be precise, I saw her in the glove department, and, to tell you the truth, I followed her." He was still liable to uncontrollable blushes. "We'd met in Suffolk, you see."

"Yes, I see." Clearly, he did.

"I caught up with her in the fur department." Once started Crankshaw wasted no time. "She was collecting a mink cape and I waited about while she talked to the salesgirl and put it on. I felt a bit of a fool, you know, but once she was leaving I went up and spoke to her. We talked a bit, and walked through to the glove department again; she left me there and I saw her go through to the main entrance – and five minutes later I found her in the manager's office accused of shoplifting."

"Did you so?"

"Yes, a frame-up if ever there was one. It was a good thing for her she had her wits about her and remembered me – I'd told her I was on duty there – or she'd have been on the spot all right. Someone – a dark-haired girl – had pointed her out to a salesgirl; said she'd seen her lift a string of pearls from the counter and put them in the pocket of her fur cape. As a matter of fact Patience – Miss Smith – didn't even know there was a pocket in the cape. She was just picking it up for a cousin of hers."

"There's no doubt it was a frame-up?"

"Not the slightest. She was actually with me when she was supposed to be being pointed out to the salesgirl and I'd been with her ever since she put on the cape. The shop detective followed her to the door and then took her straight back to the manager's office. Unless she pinched it when she was with me or when he was following her . . . well, there you are. Besides, the salesgirl in the fur department remembered a dark-haired girl trying on the cape by mistake. It's easy enough to see how it was done. But why? I just thought it was a practical joke at the time, though Miss Smith couldn't think who'd have done it to her, but now – well, it makes you think, doesn't it?"

"Yes," said the grey-haired man, looking at the worried, hopeful face across the desk. "It does make you think."

A few days later the Chief Constable of Sussex received a personal note from an old friend of his at Scotland Yard. It was brought by a pleasant-looking, fair-haired young man, who introduced himself as Detective Sergeant Geoffrey Crankshaw, CID, and sat very still while the Chief Constable read his friend's letter.

'. . . To introduce Geoffrey Crankshaw . . .' he read, '. . . very promising young man . . . needs some work on the preparation of a case for trial . . . that affair at Featherstone Hall that your people handled so quickly . . . very useful experience for him . . . a favour to me . . .'

The double-edged flattery went home and the Chief Constable's eye on Crankshaw was friendly. "So you want to do some work on that affair at Featherstone Hall," he said. "A bit unusual, of course, but I expect it can be arranged. Just between you and me, we're rather short-handed just now and I think they'll be glad to have you. You want to do the full report on the case, is that right?"

"Yes, sir. If it's at all possible." Crankshaw tried not to sound too desperately in earnest.

"I'll see what I can do."

Two hours later Crankshaw found himself on his way to Featherstone Hall. Inspector Harris, who was in charge of the case, had been unfeignedly glad to see him. "Time they did realise how short-handed we are," was his comment. "To tell you the truth, there's hardly been a bit of paperwork done yet on this case; we've been too busy making our arrest." A simple man, he did not try to conceal his pride in the announcement. "I'll be delighted to have you take over the desk side. Record-keeping has always bored me to death; action is my line." A large hand clenched on the wheel of his car.

"You've actually arrested Miss Smith then?" Crankshaw managed to sound merely interested.

"Well, no; to be precise, she's held for questioning. It's easier that way, you know – " Harris enjoyed instructing the young – "the coroner feels he's been given a clear field, for one thing. But after the inquest – click." He sketched the closing of handcuffs and the car swerved slightly.

"It's as certain as that?"

"Plain as the nose on your face. I feel almost sorry for the girl in a way. You wouldn't think anyone could have been so stupid. College educated, too. I'm glad I didn't let my girls fool around with any of that stuff. Educates their minds at the expense of their common sense, that's all it does. Look at this one. The old lady took a fancy to her and left her all her money – plenty of it, too, by the look of things. You wait till you see the house: not my cup of tea, you understand, but very fancy stuff, very fancy indeed. But, as I was saying, the old girl left her the lot – pretty near broke, she was, when she came to them, too. Just the other day, that was. She was some sort of cousin they found starving and took in."

"Is that so?" Crankshaw was gladder than ever that he had said nothing about knowing Patience.

"Yes; flat broke, poor girl, so when she got left this packet and heard that the old lady never let a will stand for more than a week or so she decided she'd better do something about it. Oh, and I forgot, she tried a spot of forgery first – just couldn't wait for the cash, apparently."

"Forgery?"

"Yes; forged the old girl's signature to a cheque for fifty pounds and tried to cash it in the Black Stag in Leyning on Christmas Eve. The poor fool couldn't think of a likelier story than that the old lady had asked her to cash it for her on account of having always gone there. Of course she'd never had a thing from there – all her wines and so on came straight down from town – so there wasn't anything doing. Naturally when the news of the murder came out, they remembered and came along to us pretty quick. And, would you believe it, it turned out that old Mrs Ffeathers had missed the cheque from her book already and stopped it at the bank! There wasn't much got past her, by the sound of it."

"They remembered the number of the cheque at the Black Stag, then?"

"Well, no" – he was momentarily checked in his enthusiasm – "but the old lady had stopped one, and this one turned up: you'd bet they were the same, wouldn't you?"

"Yes, I suppose one would. What does Miss Smith say about it?"

"Sticks to her story that the old lady asked her to cash it. She must be crazy. The old thing had made her lawyer bring her down fifty pounds in cash when he made the new will; she still had forty-five pounds of it when she died. No reason in the world why she should have wanted another fifty over the holiday."

"Blackmail?" Crankshaw threw it in almost for luck.

"Paying it? Not her. She was more likely to be squeezing

it out of other people, by the sound of her. A proper old tartar, her family make her sound."

"Do they? All of them?" Crankshaw put each question casually, wondering how much longer he would get away with the cross-examination, but Harris was only too delighted to expatiate on so successful a case. This question slowed him down for a minute.

"It's a funny thing," he said, "they all tried to do the bereaved bit, but it was a pretty thin show. The only one who really did sound sorry was our Miss Smith – well, I suppose it might set her back a bit to find she really had killed the old lady. I know her kind; they build a lot of castles in the air but if one of them really materialises, they're struck all of a heap."

As an analysis of Patience, it seemed to Crankshaw singularly wide of the mark, but he let it pass. "You don't make them sound a very attractive family," he said.

"They're all right, as families go. You don't tend to see people at their best in our line of business. And you can't blame them for being upset about the money. She had it all, you know, every blessed penny."

"And she left the whole lot to Miss Smith?"

"Two hundred a year to each of the others for life; annuities for the servants; all that kind of thing done quite regularly; and all the rest to Miss Smith. It was a regular thing with her, apparently. The form of the will was always the same, it was just the main beneficiary she kept changing."

"Who had it been before Miss Smith came on the scene?"

"Some nonsense about a fifty-two letter alphabet, I believe. No wonder the family were sick."

"Was it a long time since anyone else in the family had been left it all?"

"I don't know." Harris was beginning to sound bored with this line of discussion. "But I expect Protheroe will be able to tell you. He's the family lawyer: capable man, very, and most helpful. He's another cousin, by the way, but he wasn't there on the night of the crime, so you don't have to bother too much about him."

Contrarily, Crankshaw at once resolved to bother extensively about Mr Protheroe. But there was too much ground to be covered before they got to the house. He turned to another point. "How about alibis?" he asked. "Could you eliminate most of the family right away? It was a most remarkably quick arrest, surely?"

"Detention," Harris corrected him, pride dripping through his tone. "No, as a matter of fact, the servants were pretty clearly out of it, but, aside from them, pretty well any member of the house party could have done it. In a way, that is; of course when we started to look at it closely there was a good deal more to it than that."

"Naturally." Crankshaw was all respectful attention.

"You see" – Harris was well away now – "the old lady always had an evening drink of Bovril – everyone knew it, and everyone knew that if she was extra tired or excited for any reason she had one or two sleeping pills in it. And some brandy to take the taste away."

"Brandy and Bovril and sleeping pills," said Crankshaw. "Good Lord."

"Yes; you can see she was a tough old customer. Anyway, she was a bit wrought up, it being Christmas Eve and all, and she told Miss Smith she'd have two pills in the Bovril.

I should have explained that the whole lot of them were in her room by this time; filling Christmas stockings or some nonsense of that kind. It was latish – eleven o'clock or so – they'd been playing charades earlier in the evening."

"Sounds a happy party."

"Yes" – he sounded doubtful – "it sounds cheerful enough, doesn't it, but somehow it didn't seem to have been, to hear them talk about it. Still that's natural enough, really, when you think what happened later."

"Nothing untoward happened earlier in the evening then?"

"Untoward? No. Not unless you count Miss Smith's trying to cash her dud cheque that afternoon, and laying in an extra bottle of Mrs Ffeathers' sleeping pills on a forged prescription."

"She forged a prescription, too, did she?" Never, for one moment, would he believe it.

"Yes; quite a good imitation of Dr Findlayson's hiero-glyphics; it fooled the chemist completely, but of course when we came to check up we discovered that the old lady had had a new bottle from her own chemist just the week before. It's a funny thing: the girl went to all the trouble of forging the prescription and then never used that lot of pills after all; we found the full bottle tucked in among her nylons. She just took some out of the bottle in Mrs Ffeathers' bathroom; there were a lot missing from there. She used enough, all right; far more than were necessary, the doctor said. It's amazing the old lady didn't notice the taste, but she had her Bovril black and strong, appar-ently, and what with that and the brandy – well, there you are."

"And your idea is that instead of putting in two pills, Miss

Smith shoved in a round dozen or so, is it? She always made the Bovril, did she?"

"Not exactly. The cook made it downstairs, and then Andrews, the parlour maid, brought it up when she served the after-dinner coffee and left it ready on a gas ring in Mrs Ffeathers' bathroom. But I think we can assume the stuff was all right when it was put in Mrs Ffeathers' bathroom. I've checked and rechecked on that, and it seems clear enough that no one was alone with it till then. It was a busy night in the kitchen, the cook was making coffee, the kitchen maid brewed up the Bovril on the stove right beside her. I suppose she *might* have slipped some pills in under the cook's nose, but she'd have been lucky if she'd got away with it; and I'm damned if I can think up a motive for her. Then she gave the saucepan to Andrews, who put it on the coffee tray and took it upstairs, accompanied by the butler who held the door of Mrs Ffeathers' bathroom open for her and watched her put the saucepan on the gas. If you ask me, they then paused for a spot of flirtation, but that doesn't invalidate their evidence."

"Not necessarily. But the Bovril was then left in an empty room?"

"No. That was our first real stroke of luck. Someone had spilt a great patch of ink in Mrs Ffeathers' room and after she served the coffee Andrews went back there – still accompanied by the faithful butler – and worked at getting it out until the party came upstairs. Again, I think you could prove that they took rather longer over it than was necessary, but you can't for a minute convince me they spent the time putting pills into the Bovril."

"No; I admit it's an unlikely occupation for a courting couple. And when the party came up?"

"They all came together" – Harris was warming to his climax – "and no one – I tell you no one – went into that bathroom till Miss Smith went to get the Bovril."

"Could she be seen from the room?"

"No, she was behind the open door. I've tried, of course, with them all where they sat that night, and no one could possibly have seen her, except, perhaps, Miss Priscilla Ffeathers, but she was busy pouring tea and says she didn't notice a thing."

"Tea? I thought you said coffee."

"That was earlier. The tea was by way of a night cap; and to judge by some of their expressions, not too popular a one."

"They indulged in tea while the old lady swigged away at her brandy and Bovril. Did she drink it at once, by the way?"

"No, it was on the table beside her for quite a bit – in fact, when she did drink it, she complained it was cold. But you're not going to tell me anyone dropped in a handful of pills in the middle of that crowded room are you? The only person who had a ghost of a chance was Miss Priscilla Ffeathers who sat by the old lady pouring tea, but she had nowhere she could have carried them; the ladies were all in evening dress."

"Hadn't she a bag?"

"No, she hadn't. I got the impression she was a bit hard up – Mrs Ffeathers kept some of them pretty short of cash – and just hadn't got an evening one. The girl who searched her room said she hadn't a thing she could have carried with the dress she wore."

"Nobody else went near the cup?"

"I wouldn't put it quite so strongly as that. Various people went over to talk to the old lady in the course of the evening: Joseph Ffeathers, Mrs Brigance, her son Mark Brigance and Seward Ffeathers, but so far as I can work it out somebody was watching each of them all the time. It stands to reason the old lady would be the centre of attention and anyone who went over to talk to her would be watched – casually, you know, but they wouldn't have had a chance of doctoring her drink. Besides, what about her? Everyone agrees she was sharp as they come – don't you think she'd have noticed?"

"Yes." Crankshaw's heart sank within him. Not, he hastened to reassure himself, that there was the slightest chance Patience could have done it, but she had certainly managed to get herself into an extraordinarily uncomfortable position.

"You could see at once *they* all thought she'd done it," Harris was summing up triumphantly. "They didn't want to say anything, but I got it out of them gradually. You know how it comes, a bit here and a bit there. I was pretty sure, really, before there was anything you could call evidence at all. There was the motive, large as life. Money, poor girl, and lots of it. Oh, they tried to keep it quiet about her being broke; Mrs Brigance, who'd hired her, kept going on about what a favour she'd done them by coming, but – well, I won't pretend I was surprised when I heard about the forged prescription and cheque. Pleased, yes – I've seldom had a case so tidy – but not surprised." He slowed the car to turn off the main road. "But here we are. I hope I've given you a bit of an idea of what it's all about."

"You certainly have. I hardly feel I need to come here at all, I've got it all so clearly in my head."

"That's fine, but mind you feel free to run around and ask all the questions you please, to fill in the background. It's not often we get help from the Yard like this, and I want to do right by you."

Crankshaw thanked him with an inward quirk of conscience at the thought of how far from right by Harris his own intentions were.

The car had passed through wrought iron gates hung from high pillars, each with its ornamental granite ball, and turned up a well-kept drive. Soon Featherstone Hall stood before them in all its Victorian surfeit of ornamentation, its red brick front excrescent with domes, turrets, cupolas and here and there an unnecessary pillar holding yet another granite ball. Crankshaw cast one shocked glance upwards, then followed Harris into the equally alarming modernity of the white and chromium front hall. A parlour maid, presumably Andrews, took their coats, sniffed slightly at Harris and flashed a quick, interested glance at Crankshaw.

Reflecting gloomily on the snobbery of the working classes, he reminded himself that her obvious respect for his decently ancient tweeds would doubtless smooth his path when he interviewed her. If he got the chance to do so, which seemed unlikely, with Harris so very much in command. He fought down a moment's desperate vision of Patience in her cell and followed Harris into a large and bookless library. A bluff, bewhiskered semi-military man rose to greet them from the large desk where he was sorting papers. "Ah, Harris, back again so soon?"

The remark was hardly welcoming, but Harris chose to ignore this. He introduced Crankshaw to Joseph Ffeathers, explaining that he was to compile the official report on the case. "I'm afraid I'll have to ask you to put up with a few more questions, just till Mr Crankshaw gets things clear. He's just joined us, you see, from Scotland Yard."

"Is that so?" Joseph Ffeathers looked at once sceptical at Crankshaw's youth and impressed at his origin. "Does this mean you are not . . . I believe the phrase would be 'satisfied'? I should be glad to hear that poor young Patience was well out of it."

The remark rang curiously false to Crankshaw's sensitive ear, but Harris seemed to notice nothing. "Oh, no, not that." He was bland, almost soothing. "I don't think there's much doubt we've got the guilty party – speaking quite off the record, you understand. But of course we have to have it all shipshape for the inquest, and Crankshaw here is going to take care of the routine for us. To tell you the truth" – he obviously found Ffeathers sympathetic – "we're a bit short-handed right now and if this young fellow hadn't come along I don't know how we'd have got our case together for Friday."

Crankshaw felt himself patronised, resented it, and at the same time reminded himself that the more innocuous he seemed, the better were his chances of getting under somebody's guard. If he only knew whose . . .

"So the inquest's Friday, is it? That's quick work. Well, of course we'd hoped the questioning and so forth was all over with, but naturally we'll do all we can to cooperate with Mr – er – Crimshaw. I just hope he'll go easy with the womenfolk; they're all pretty well on edge, as you can imagine."

Ffeathers had cast himself, Crankshaw thought, as one of Kipling's Indian colonels, though surely underneath the façade there lurked something a good deal more intelligent, and very likely less trustworthy . . . But it was too early to be more than generally suspicious.

Harris was looking at his watch. "I must be on my way. You may think yours is the only crime in Sussex, but it's not by a long way. Let me have a report when you get back tonight, Crankshaw."

On that, with perhaps the faintest of malicious twinkles, he was gone. Sink or swim, thought Crankshaw; but it suited him well enough.

The pseudo-colonel was looking at him from under bushy brows. "First job, eh? We'll do all we can to help. Now, where do you want to begin?"

"Perhaps at the beginning," suggested Crankshaw mildly. He pulled a solid, straight-backed chair up to the wrong side of the desk, cleared a space for himself and opened his notebook.

"Oh, the beginning. Well, I suppose you'd say that was the week before Christmas, when we heard poor Patience Smith was broke – she's a kind of cousin of ours, you know."

"Yes, so I understand. But that is not just what I meant by the beginning." Crankshaw looked at the older man, very much at his ease against the chimney-piece, and waited.

"Oh, I see. You want it *ab ovum*, as the curate said." Was the laugh a shade too hearty? "Would my mother's birth be far enough back for you?"

"I think that would do nicely." So far Crankshaw had written nothing, but now, deliberately, he took up his pen, wrote 'Mrs Ffeathers' in very beautiful script, underlined it and looked up at Ffeathers.

"Right. Here goes then. Born 1859 of poor and not too

honest parents. She rather boasted about her father's goings-on, but then she boasted about so much, poor Mother." It was the first genuine note he had achieved. "Early life very much what you'd expect," he went on. "One semi-slum after another, Grandfather drinking when he had the money, beating his wife when he hadn't. Am I being detailed enough for you?"

"Quite, thank you." Crankshaw welcomed the note of mockery. "I understand that your mother had very considerable success on the stage."

"Music halls, you mean. She was a riot. She's got a great trunkful upstairs: programmes, ads – *billets doux* generally. You can go through it if you like; it gives you a pretty good idea of the times she had. I've always admired Mother, she was a great girl." Again, it rang true.

"Yes, I see. And how long was she on the stage?"

"Fifteen years. The fifteen best years of her life, she always said. Then she retired – it was a pretty hot pace she had to keep up and I don't think she really regretted giving it up as much as she used to let on."

"Retired to be married, I suppose?"

"Oh, good Lord no. She'd been married for years. Father was her – well, I suppose you'd call him her agent these days; her fixer generally. He discovered her, way back, in a pub in Seven Dials singing sea shanties with her father. He got her her first part and when she clicked, well, he married her. I expect it was the safest way for an agent to get his cut in those days. But he'd died before she retired. There were—" he coughed, hesitated "—various relationships. She used to tell the most amazing tales, did Mother. Some of them may even have been true. But she did like to shock people."

"Yes, I see. So what year did she retire?"

Ffeathers hesitated. "Damned if I can remember. I expect
Josephine will, or my brother Seward. He was born in 1890.
I do know that because he made a bit of a song and dance
about his sixtieth birthday. So I expect they were married in
1889, if I know Mother. She was never one to let the grass
grow under her feet."

Crankshaw did his best to look shocked. "Your brother
Seward is the oldest of you then?"

"Yes. There was a gap after him. I expect he interfered
with her career more than she'd expected. I wasn't born
till 1900."

"And your sister?"

"In 1902. She's a mere chicken, Josephine. Good idea
to get it straight from me, come to think of it. She'd tell
you 1910."

Crankshaw made another note, amused at the effort
Ffeathers was making to get back into the role of bluff
colonel out of which he had slipped a bit in the course
of the interview. "I see," he said. "I understand that Mr
Brigance is dead, and that your and your brother's wives
live here. So that takes care of your generation. Now for
the next one."

"Five deplorable grandchildren, Mother would have told
you. Two of Seward's: Ludwig and Leonora, poor creatures.
He intended them for musicians, but they're chemistry-mad
instead. They've got a room at the back of the house
I'd advise you to keep out of if you don't want to suffo-
cate. Two of Josephine's: Mark and Mary, decent enough
youngsters, good-looking, bright enough. Mark did well
at Cambridge, Mary's got a job, interior decorating or

something, and a flat in town. Her fiancé's staying here, you know; Tony Wetherall – if he has the nerve to go through with it. They only announced it on Christmas Eve."

"Bad luck, that," said Crankshaw, and then, as the pause prolonged itself, "And your family?"

"One girl, Priscilla. That's the lot."

"The entire Christmas house party?"

"Yes – no, there was a young fool called Duguid, Brian Duguid, my wife asked down for Priss. I could have told her that was no good."

Not for the first time in the interview Crankshaw registered surprise at how much he was being told. But no doubt far more of the iceberg, truth, was still submerged. "Good," he said. "So much for the house party. Now, if you wouldn't mind just taking me through what happened on Christmas Eve, I don't think I'll need to trouble you any further."

"But you've forgotten Miss Smith. I mean, I don't like to drag her in, but of course she was here too."

"Yes, of course; stupid of me. She is a cousin, I understand?"

"More or less; Mother's sister's granddaughter. Her parents died when she was a child and she lived with us for a bit. Seward and another cousin, Paul Protheroe – you'll meet him, he's Mother's lawyer – are her trustees. Not that there's anything left in the trust, poor kid. It's no wonder she went haywire. D'you think they'll be able to make it unsound mind?"

"That," said Crankshaw, "is hardly my affair." He hurried on to conceal the anger that charged him. "She had only been here ten days, is that right?"

"Yes. When we heard about her money being gone,

Josephine suggested we get her down for Mother – two birds with one stone, you know. Just between you and me, Mother was a bit of a tartar, and companions never stayed."

"But she liked Miss Smith well enough to leave her all her money?"

"Oh, Lord bless you, that didn't mean anything. Everyone she met had it left to them at one time or other. She'd run through all of us, and been playing the same game on charities. Less entertaining though, because they weren't around to suffer over it. She was threatening to cut Patience off already. I heard her. I suppose that's what drove the poor kid dotty – she was really broke, you know; stony. It's a bad business Crankshaw, a bad sad business."

"Murder is." Crankshaw's hand shook as he wrote the note that might help to hang Patience. But keep calm, keep calm. "Now for the events of Christmas Eve." The formal language steadied him.

"Well, let me see. Nothing out of the way till dinner. Nothing much then, for the matter of that, but I expect you want everything."

"Of course." Crankshaw took extensive notes while Joseph described the formal dinner, the charades and then the moving of the party up to his mother's room. "She liked us to fill the stockings up there, y'know. They hung from her mantelshelf." The account was accurate enough except that it omitted all mention of the stolen five pounds and Mrs Ffeathers' threat of a momentous announcement in the course of the evening.

"Thank you," said Crankshaw when he had finished. "And

105

in your opinion no one could have drugged the Bovril once it was in Mrs Ffeathers' room?"

"That's right." Joseph was positive. "The only one with a ghost of a chance was my poor Priss and you can bet your last penny she didn't. Besides, where'd she have carried the stuff? She'd no bag to go with her dress; I know because my wife was after me to give her one for Christmas. Lot of female nonsense."

That seemed to be all that was to be got from Joseph Ffeathers, and Crankshaw thanked him again and asked if he might interview the rest of the party. "In any order that's convenient. I don't want it to be any more trouble than it has to be." He forestalled Joseph's complaint.

Josephine came first. Voluble and exclamatory, she added little to what Crankshaw already knew. Only, probing behind her words, he felt that where Joseph would gladly have Patience hanged and the whole thing over with as quickly as possible, Josephine had some curious, semi-conscious uncertainty about Patience's guilt. She insisted again and again that the legacy to Patience was not necessarily a passing fancy: "She adored Patience, you know, simply adored her at sight. We were all quite green with envy. Patience needn't have worried, she'd have been all right . . ." And much more on the same theme, which became more comprehensible to Crankshaw when he interviewed her son and daughter.

Mary came first, accompanied, at her request, by Tony Wetherall. She wore a black dress and a brave little air of 'no secrets' that obviously pleased Tony. Plunging at once into the middle of things, she begged Crankshaw to be gentle with her brother. "Poor Mark is in a frightful stew," she explained. And with a conspiratorial glance at Crankshaw, youth appealing to youth: "That man Harris absolutely chewed him up."

"He minds very much, your brother?" To an extent, Crankshaw met the appeal.

"Dreadfully. Not so much about Gran," she went on, with the realism of her age and sex. "Of course, it's wretched about her, and we all feel it, but after all she was ninety-one. She'd had quite a run."

"Yes," said Crankshaw. "So I understand."

Another conspirator's glance. "How she loved to talk about it," Mary digressed. "To shock people, you know. She used to have Priss and Leonora absolutely crimson – and Ludwig too. I remember she tried it on Patience the first night, but she was a tough one. No blushes there. I think that's when Gran began to take to her. I don't think Patience did it, you know. She has more sense." It was almost an aside, casual and unemphatic. "But Mark seems to think she did. He was rather taken with her, more than he admitted, I think. Rather funny, that, when you think about it." She did not explain why. "Poor old Mark, he never did have much sense. Brains, you know, but not sense."

Interviewing Mark, Crankshaw was inclined to agree. He paced, he prowled, he lit cigarettes and abandoned them, sat down and got up again to pace and prowl some more, until Crankshaw could gladly have shaken him for what seemed almost a travesty of his own ferocious anxiety. He became, as the questions and answers went on, more and more convinced that Mark Brigance knew something absolutely damning, but would rather die than admit it. His manner in the witness box would be disastrous for Patience,

Crankshaw thought, and dismissed him for the time being, his burden of anxiety heavier than ever.

Seward and his ailing wife had nothing to add to the story of the evening, but managed to convey so cold an impression of fear that Crankshaw relegated them, too, to the mental limbo where Mark awaited further consideration. Something was worrying them badly, but he was not at all sure if it had anything to do with the murder. About that they were drearily positive, and on the note of 'poor Patience' and a flood of invalid's easy tears he dismissed them.

Priss followed them, pale and red-nosed. Like Mary, she refused to believe in Patience's guilt. "It can't be true. I liked her." Crankshaw had the impression that she did not like many people.

But under questioning she could only confirm the impossibility of anyone's drugging the Bovril under her eyes. It had been across the table from her, beyond the tea tray. Yes, people had been going to and fro with cups, but she would have been sure to notice. "You know, you watch people when you are serving them. Besides, there was Gran. She didn't miss much, I can tell you."

"And I gather you had nowhere you could have carried the pills?" He put it to her straight.

She raised red-rimmed eyes to his. "No. Lucky for me, wasn't it? I did hope Dad would give me a bag for Christmas, but now I'm glad he didn't. I had a foul cold, too; I had to borrow Leonora's handkerchief."

"Had she a bag?"

"Yes, but she couldn't have . . . Oh, how horrible it all is!" She dripped into tears and he let her go.

Leonora confirmed the loan of the handkerchief. She

had asked to be interviewed with her brother and turned to him for confirmation. "You remember, Ludwig, she never returned it – just like her – and I had to borrow yours later on."

"Yes," said Ludwig, "that's right. But anyway, we've got to face it; it's obvious poor Patience did it." To the best of his ability, he was the man of the world. "I really think, Leo, you ought to tell Mr Crankshaw what you heard that night."

"Oh dear." Leonora hesitated. "It seems so mean. After all, it was an accident. I oughtn't to have heard really." She looked forlornly from her brother to Crankshaw.

"Better tell me," said Crankshaw kindly. "It will get it off your mind, for one thing."

"It seems so kind of sneaky." Not long out of school, so might she have discussed reporting an erring classmate to the headmistress. "You see, I was waiting for Ludwig at the top of the stairs, just outside Granny's door, on Christmas Eve, and I couldn't help hearing her talking to Patience – she was absolutely shrieking at her. 'I'll have the police on you,' she said." Leonora stopped and gazed at Crankshaw, half frightened, half triumphant.

"Just a minute." He fought down cold panic. "How do you know it was Miss Smith Mrs Ffeathers was talking to?"

"She called her Patience." An unmistakable note of satisfaction.

"Yes, that does seem to settle it." It did indeed. Crankshaw dismissed them, wondering what further damning evidence against Patience his last interview, with Paul Protheroe, would produce.

Protheroe sat himself down opposite Crankshaw, took his watch out of his pocket, looked at it gloomily and put it down on the table in front of him. Having thus made his position clear he was helpfulness itself. "The details of the will. Yes, of course. Simple enough as a matter of fact. They were all the same, you know, except for the major legatee. Mrs Ffeathers had her faults, but . . . It's odd, come to think of it; she was too much of a lady to play around with her bequests to the servants and so on. It was her family she tormented."

"She put them through it?"

"She certainly did. Though, mark you, it was getting a bit stale with them. There'd been so many dramatic deletions and epic restorations that I think they'd all got pretty well used to it. I've noticed the last few times I've been down that the scenes weren't half so tense as they used to be."

"That's interesting. You came down every time she changed her will?"

"Yes. A great nuisance it was too. But I'm a kind of cousin of theirs, so it seemed only decent. And, besides" – an admirable display of manly frankness – "it was good business for the firm."

"I suppose so. You say the family were less worried about the will lately. Does that mean that they were not entirely dependent on Mrs Ffeathers?"

"Not at all. Oh, her children all have small incomes of their own, but nothing they could possibly manage on without her help."

"Then isn't it rather odd they took it all so calmly?"

"I don't think so. I think that between them they must have decided it really was just a game and that when it came to the point she'd do the decent thing. Or else that whoever got the lot would divide it with the others."

110

"And was there such a will?"

"What do you mean?"

"A reasonably fair one, tucked away somewhere. To be dusted off and ratified when she felt like it."

"Oh, I see what you mean. There have been so many. And I did always try and see to it that she destroyed her copies of the old ones. But that wasn't my point. I think what they were counting on was some kind of a deathbed change of heart. Of course they weren't to know she would go off in her sleep like that, poor old dear."

"Just so," said Crankshaw. "So what you are saying is that her dying like that was very much against their interest."

"My point exactly." Protheroe glanced discreetly at his watch. "Is there anything else I can tell you?"

"I hope so. Your firm also handled Miss Smith's affairs, I believe?"

"We did all the family business. Miss Smith's grand-mother was Mrs Ffeathers' younger sister, you know. She had just the one daughter – Angelina, I believe she was called – who married a very up-and-coming young man called Smith. He made a packet in the City, though I'd rather not think too closely about how he did it. They both died when Miss Smith, their only daughter, was eleven. Seward Ffeathers and I were left as trustees and guardians, for our sins. That was a foolish will if ever there was one. Some sharp city friend of Smith's must have drawn it up for him, too clever by half. Well, Smith, being the self-made man he was, never would trust anyone's judgment but his own. He left the money so tied up that Ffeathers and I could do practically nothing but pay out the income he had stipulated for his daughter. And of course, poor fellow, he hadn't allowed for dying so young – people never do, I find – and what with that and the double death duties, and then the total collapse of some mining stock he had gone in for pretty heavily . . ." He paused for a moment, staring unhappily into the fire, then went on. "Of course we kept hoping they would recover; you never can tell with these mining ventures and I for one had a good deal of respect for Smith's judgement so far as the stock market was concerned. Anyway, I'm afraid we went on paying Miss Smith's income cheques rather longer than we should have. Of course the firm will back it, especially in the case of this family, but it's an awkward business all round. I had the unpleasant task of breaking it to poor Miss Smith just ten days before Christmas. Lord, what a long time ago it seems now. Poor girl, if I'd only had any idea of what would come of it. I know it's ridiculous, but I can't help blaming myself."

"For what, exactly?"

"Why, for suggesting she come down here as Mrs Ffeathers' companion. Mrs Brigance came in just when I'd realised we'd come to the end so far as poor Miss Smith was concerned. Josephine was in despair because the latest companion had just left in a tantrum, so I suggested she give Miss Smith a trial. And, my God, look what's come of it. I can't get it out of my mind." He took another glance at his watch. "By the way, I forgot to tell you that Brian Duguid is very anxious to be interviewed as soon as you can manage. He's got a telephone call coming through or something."

"Duguid? Good Lord, I'd forgotten all about him." If not exactly true, it was near enough. "Perhaps you'd be so good as to ask him to come in next." Protheroe had risen, but

Crankshaw held him for a moment. "By the way, what was the name of the mining company?"

"Miss Smith's?" Protheroe looked surprised but tolerant. "I'd always heard the Yard was thorough. Let me think, what were they called? Consolidated Elephants or something. I'll check up for you when I get back to the office if you like."

"Thank you."

Protheroe got as far as the door, then turned. "Look," he said, "one other thing. I don't know if you'll be seeing Miss Smith, but if you do, I would be grateful if you'd persuade her to let me get her a lawyer. She wouldn't hear of it the other day; I expect she hadn't taken things in yet; but the right man from the start might make all the difference—" He stopped there. More clearly than words his tone conveyed that the difference would be between hanging and a life sentence.

"I'll see what I can do." Crankshaw was glad to see the last of this too confident young man, without, he hoped, having betrayed just how angry he had made him.

Brian Duguid, diffident and agitated, came as something of a relief. He had nothing to add except an impression, strongly conveyed, that the whole family were crazy. 'And I might have spent Christmas at the Cholmondelys' was his refrain, and Crankshaw dismissed him with a sardonic, "Why didn't you?"

It was time to be going. A wild December wind had banked clouds around the house and darkened the sky even before mid-winter's nightfall. Crankshaw's head ached and so, though he refused to admit it, did his heart. Of course Patience was innocent. There had been a conspiracy against her, or some equally diabolical chain of unlucky chance. When he saw her, she would resolve it all. But he was afraid to see her. Patience, guilty? Faced, the thought was intolerable. He snapped his notebook shut and went out into the twilit hall. Josephine Brigance hovered there, waiting for him. "Your car is here for you, but perhaps a cup of tea? You've had a long day."

"No, thanks very much. I must be getting back." He hated this house.

But it was hard to get away: Joseph appeared for a minute at the drawing room door to ask if he had finished, and looked glum at the news that he had not and would return next day, "For a few odd points."

Mary came in at the front door as he was about to open it, windblown and rain-sprinkled. She said something explanatory about dogs, then caught his arm. "When you see Patience, you'll remember to give her my love?"

Unwillingly, he let the door shut again between him and the free night outside, and paused to answer her, aware as he did so of Josephine still hovering disapprovingly. "Of course I will." His heart warmed to her, the first person who seemed to believe Patience innocent.

Outside, the air struck cold after the overheated house. He stood for a minute, his eyes adjusting to the darkness and his mind focusing on the little group he had left behind in the hall. Joseph had looked cross, Mary had looked anxious, but what had the look been on Josephine's face? Anxiety was making him imagine things. High time he got back to Leyning to start his report and clear his mind by doing so. He took a gloomy look at the weather, buttoned up his coat and stepped out of the porch towards the waiting car.

The moment's hesitation saved his life. As he stepped forward he heard a grinding roar from above, paused instinctively, and saw an enormous mass fall on the drive in front of him. Inside the house, someone screamed.

Part Two

1998

Seven

Turning the key in the still unfamiliar lock, Patience felt the sense of liberation that she always experienced on coming to this house: her house, as Featherstone Hall had never quite been. Too many ghosts there, she thought, closing the door behind her. Ghosts of the resentful living, too; much more threatening than the unknown dead.

She hung her coat on one of the old-fashioned brass hooks she had rescued from the cellar and took her shopping through to the combined kitchen and dining room at the back of the house. It was the first fresh food she had brought into her new home, and tonight she would sleep in the new bed upstairs for the first time. No hostility here; surely that was all left behind at Featherstone Hall. Not that one could blame Mrs Ffeathers' family for being outraged at seeing the fortune they had counted on snatched away. As next of kin, they would have shared the old lady's estate if she had been found guilty of her murder and so unable to inherit. Thinking of that time could still make her shiver.

A patch of autumn sun slanted across the bench she had put on the small patch of grass at the back of the house. She poured a glass of sherry and took it out there, raised the glass to the cobbled back of her new home and drank a silent toast. To freedom. She had escaped again. Though, looking back, she hardly blamed Inspector Harris for believing her guilty that first time. The evidence was so strong against her that, sitting in the cold cell where she was being 'held for questioning', she had seen the gallows looming. And then Geoffrey had arrived, St George to the rescue. His belief in her innocence had shone like sunshine in that bleak little room, a warm relief after the shock of Mark's turning against her. Something had frozen in her when she saw that he was part of that hostile little family group. She had so very nearly accepted him, the night before. She would never trust instinct again.

She had started to thaw under Geoffrey's sympathetic questioning, and felt her mind begin to work again. Together, they had set about untying the knots of evidence that bound her. It was she herself, in fact, who had first suggested the possibility that it might be one last gigantic, sick joke on old Mrs Ffeathers' part.

Geoffrey had seized on the idea and set to work to unravel the damning evidence, stitch by stitch. A handwriting expert had agreed that the signature on the £50 cheque was most probably Mrs Ffeathers' own. She had forged her own signature so as to get a hold on Patience. And a search of her room had produced some more stolen prescription blanks, carefully concealed in the bible she boasted she never read. Most important of all, Dr Findlayson had admitted, under Geoffrey's friendly, casual questioning, that the old lady had, in fact, been worried about what she was convinced were the first signs of senile dementia.

"But what an unbelievably wicked thing to do," Geoffrey had said, reporting this to Patience, still in her cell, but very much more cheerful. "To kill herself and let the evidence point to you."

"I think she was wicked," Patience had told him. "Look what she had done to her children: ruined their lives; kept them as prisoners, to torment. And I resisted her. I was going to get away, at whatever cost. I hadn't told her yet, but I know she felt it." It was all true. Was it the whole truth? At least it had worked. She had been released by a red-faced, apologetic Inspector Harris before the inquest, but had refused to go back to Featherstone Hall.

"They ganged up on me," she had explained, when Geoffrey thought this unwise. "It was horrible. All of them. I'm sorry. I don't want to see any of them until this is all over. If then. I don't even want to talk about it." She would not let herself think about Mark.

Infinitely supportive, Geoffrey had found her a room, not at the Black Stag, and a Leyning solicitor, Mr Jones, when she had said she did not want Paul Protheroe. "You're a rich woman," Geoffrey had reminded her. "You can take your pick."

It was getting cold. The sun had gone in. She went into her shining new kitchen and assembled bread and cheese, salad and fruit for lunch. Delightful not to be waited on. That was one of all the many things she had disliked about living at Featherstone Hall. And yet she had lived there for almost fifty years. Unbelievable. But Geoffrey had wanted to. She nibbled Stilton and remembered the inquest, with the solid ranks of Ffeatherses and Brigances gazing inimically at her across the hall, and the by then inevitable verdict of suicide while of unsound mind. Afterwards, she had gone on refusing to see them.

Geoffrey had not approved of this. "Better get it over with," he had urged. "You'll have to one day."

"Why?" she had asked, still refusing to think about Mark.

Mr Jones, the solicitor from the firm Mrs Ffeathers had not dealt with in Leyning, had protested at the settlements she insisted on making on the family, but she had been adamant. "It should have gone to them really," she told him. "She never meant that will to stand. And more than anything I want to make a clean break, feel free of them. This way, I can."

She had said the same thing to Geoffrey, also protesting, and had refused to let him reopen the odd business of the attempt to frame her for shoplifting. "I'm sure it has to have been one of the girls," she told him, "Mary or Leonora or Priss, but I would much rather not know which. Or why, come to that. It's all over, done with; I want to leave it that way."

He had been glad enough to let it go. She had, by then, a feeling that he was in bad odour back at the Yard for his enthusiastic espousal of her cause, and it made her more grateful to him than ever. "'Reader, I married him',," she quoted to herself now, and poured a second glass of sherry. Freed at last by his death, of a stroke, on the golf course one bright morning of early spring, she had found time and strength to face just what a disaster that hasty marriage had been.

She should at least have gone back to college and taken her degree. Grown up. They would have had her; they had said so. But Geoffrey had talked her out of it. "I want to take you away from it all," he had urged. "From the whole sordid business, the headlines, the gossip. Time enough when we get back to decide what to do about the Hall."

"Oh, I want to get rid of it," she had said at once, but he had been lovingly urgent that she make no more of what he called her 'rash decisions' until the prolonged honeymoon was over.

Idiotic not to have realised what their long absence must mean in terms of his career. But there had been so much to come to terms with, in those desperately difficult weeks of getting to know the near stranger she had married. Full of guilt at feeling she did not satisfy him in bed, she thought she must have failed to listen to what he was saying to her. It was only when he casually suggested that they stay another week on their Caribbean beach that she came to and protested: "But your job, Geoffrey? You must have used up all your leave for the next several years already."

"Oh that! Surely I told you, love? I packed it in. They were so stuffy about it all; it was a pleasure to throw their offer of a whole extra week back in their fat faces. You should have seen their jaws drop."

"Geoffrey, you did that for me! But, what will you do? Your career . . . Oh, I feel dreadful."

"No need to fret. I've got a much better idea." She had learned already to recognise the tone of voice that meant he had made up his mind. "We are going home to Featherstone Hall, my sweet, and I am going for a new career. I'm going to turn the tables and boss the bureaucrats for a change. Just between you and me, I'd had enough of form filling and pen pushing at the Yard. I'm for politics. It's the career I always aimed for, you know, but first I had to earn my living."

"And now you don't need to! Of course; I never thought. But, oh, Geoffrey, not Featherstone Hall."

He had taken her to bed, and talked her round. Sussex was full of safe Conservative seats, he had explained as she lay, exhausted, in his arms.

"Conservative?" That had been a surprise too, though she was not much of a political animal, then.

"Of course," he had said. "And the Hall is the perfect setting. We'll need to make some changes, naturally. All that dreadful chrome and white must go. You'll enjoy turning it back into the kind of house it ought to be, and you'll feel quite different about it when you have finished."

So many mistakes. She rose wearily and stacked dishes in the sink. She had indeed done her best to make the house and herself into the proper setting for a rising young politician, and he had plunged into local politics, eager to be co-opted on to any committee that would have him. As soon as the house was ready, she found herself busy giving dinners for his contacts, and coffee mornings for Conservative ladies. It had been a kind of game at first, and she had enjoyed playing it well, happy to feel that she was making up to him for the ways she felt she failed him.

The telephone rang. She dropped the duster with which she had been polishing the mahogany table and moved over to pick it up, wondering who it could be. She had insisted on a new number, and few people knew it yet. But when she gave her number only silence answered. "Leyning three-six-four two-four-two," she said again and was answered by a click at the other end. Whoever it was had hung up: a wrong number.

At least it had distracted her from a gloomy enough

line of thought. What use to brood over past mistakes? She found her gardening gloves and went out to start the autumn digging of her two small flower beds, delighted to be able to do it herself after all the years of gardeners who listened to her instructions and then did their own thing.

The sun went on shining; a robin came and watched her; she found she was singing tunelessly to herself as she worked, something she had not done for years. It was this secret garden, as much as the compact little house, that had won her at first sight, soon after Geoffrey had died. Terrified of losing it, she had bought the house at once, at auction, without a survey, though Mr Jones, her lawyer, had spoken gloomily of dry rot and inroads on her capital. She had defied him and never regretted it, though in fact that was when she had first realised how her huge inheritance had shrunk over the years of Geoffrey's management. It had provided her with a good, public reason for selling the Hall. One thing she had learned over the years was a healthy respect for the Leyning grapevine, and it had not failed her in this instance. She was soon meeting sympathetic looks from women who had heard of her straitened circumstances and thought them worse than they were. It was the perfect reason for extricating herself gently but firmly from her commitments to the Conservative Party. No need to live that lie any longer. It had been a lie ever since Anthony Eden's shabby handling of the Suez crisis. She had quietly voted Liberal ever since, grateful for the secret ballot and ashamed at deceiving Geoffrey. But what else could she do?

The telephone rang. She dropped her gardening gloves on the little iron table and hurried indoors to answer it, only to get the same silence, the same click. Tiresome. But she had done enough gardening. Her back was reminding her of the years she preferred to ignore. Exercise, the osteopath had said, and she had added the ones he advised to those she had learned in self-defence classes at college. She went back to the garden to do them in the sunshine, happy all over again in its privacy.

Walking was good, too. Back in the house, she combed short grey hair at the hall mirror, slapped on lipstick and a dash of pressed powder, put her keys and a ten pound note in her pocket and went out into the little town where she had chosen to live.

The house itself was so quiet that it was always a surprise to emerge directly down three steps on to the High Street, but then this, too, was quiet enough, since the shopping centre had moved to the other end of town, where Tesco was. It had been disconcerting to find, when she moved in, that the butcher, greengrocer and invaluable all-purpose store that had been round the corner when she bought the house had vanished. But you could get milk at the paper shop, she had discovered, and anyway the walk to Tesco was good for her, though she did not much like supermarkets.

It no longer surprised her to see two Conservative ladies nipping across the road to avoid her. It was not just because of her defection from the party. She had realised, early on, that people simply could not cope with the fact of bereavement, particularly not a sudden one, like hers. How long did one continue a pariah? she wondered, and remembered her friend Penelope Cunningham – only, of course, she had been Penelope Forsham by then – describing her own experience as a recent widow up in Essex. 'They drop you, you know, once you're not a couple any more. It hurts, but you get used to it.' Penelope had solved her own problem by going to live with her rich brother Gerald, who had never married and lived in extreme comfort in the south of France. Patience had gone to stay with them for a while after Geoffrey's death, but it had not worked. She sighed, remembering. She must write to dear Penelope. She turned briskly into the Post Office to buy airmail paper and stamps.

Putting the change into her pocket she crossed the road and started up the long steep track that led to her favourite view of the sea. This was the way she had come, all those years ago, when Mrs Ffeathers had sent her into Leyning with the cheque and forged prescription. She was not going to let it be haunted for her. Aside from anything else, it was much the quickest way into real country, and the driest when the weather got bad. She could not afford ghosts here, nor to be reminded of the niggling doubt that had always lurked in the back of her mind after that convenient verdict.

It was dusk when she got home, and it felt more like home than ever as she drew the curtains in the front hall against High Street eyes and put on the kettle for a cup of tea. No need to draw curtains at the back of the house. One of its great virtues for her were the high flint walls on each side of the long garden and the creeper-hung one at the end where the lane cut her off from the graveyard beyond. When she had finished the flower beds she must make a start on cutting back the polygonum that had taken over that end wall. She might even find that she needed experts to do it, but hoped to manage it herself. Already she felt it her garden as the one at Featherstone Hall had never been, but it had inevitably been neglected in the months when she had had to stay on at the Hall, settling the estate and arranging the sale.

It had been a lonely time, lonelier even than she had expected. She had been angry with herself at finding she had so few friends. You don't make friends when you are living a lie, she thought now, and she had been living at least two. Three really. She had pretended to be the happily married wife of a successful politician, and that she shared his politics. None of it true. He was not even successful. She had recognised this finally, too late, at the meeting where he was not selected as prospective parliamentary candidate for the district. That was a long time ago – but she remembered it with cruel clarity. The other candidate had spoken first, and spoken well, and then Geoffrey had stood up and got it all just faintly, fatally wrong. He had been sure and unsure of himself in all the wrong places and she had known it for a lost cause when he sat down.

Afterwards, he had blamed her, and in some ways, though not the ones he accused her of, he had been right. She had failed him because the gap between his thinking and hers had become so wide that it had been impossible for them to discuss things. Instead, she had cravenly taken to agreeing with him so as to avoid the rages he got into when she did not. Cavilling, he called it. After that bitterly disappointing failure, he had been away from home, on one pretext or another, more than ever, and it had been nothing but a relief to her. But she had been lonely. And here she was now, in her new house, with no close friend on whom she could rely, no one who would telephone and ask how she was settling. My fault, she thought. I must join things, non-political things: the University of the Third Age, the local theatre company, groups like that. How else would one meet one's neighbours, now the age of the morning call was past?

128

On the thought, the front door bell rang, surprisingly loud in the small house. It was dark now. Should she put the chain on? It seemed idiotic, here in the High Street. She switched on the outside light and opened the door.

There was nobody there. She looked up and down the surprisingly empty street. Nothing. Had she really taken so long to get to the door, or had it simply been a naughty child, ringing and running? Probably.

She went back into the kitchen to put a chop into the oven for her supper, irked with herself at letting the incident upset her. But it had left her jumpy. Idiotic, but she suddenly found she did not like the feel of the black garden outside, and drew the curtains there too. That felt better.

She got out table mats and silver to set a proper table – begin as you mean to go on – and the telephone rang. She did not even expect a voice this time, and there was none. I'll ring the operator in the morning, she thought; this is beyond a joke.

In the morning, taking out bread for the robin, she saw footprints in the newly dug flower bed. Not her own; she knew that at once. Her walking shoes left an unmistakable pattern in the soft earth, but these were the marks of trainers, and smaller ones than hers. Impossible. But they were here, in the little bed under the kitchen window where she meant to plant sweet-william for the scent. No wonder she had felt nervous last night. Someone had been standing there, watching her.

It was impossible, but it seemed to be true. She looked up at the high walls on either side of her garden. Hard to imagine either of her neighbours getting out a long ladder and manoeuvring it over the wall. Mrs Palmer on the right hand had lived in her little house all her long life and was letting it fall quietly to ruin around her. Mr Simpson, on the other side, had only moved in since Patience had bought and never seemed to be at home at all. He worked in the City, she knew, and commuting from Leyning must be no joke. She had recognised early on that neither of them would be the kind of useful neighbour who takes in parcels and messages, and had been glad that she owned the wall between her garden and Mrs Palmer's neglected one. Anyway, there were no ladder marks in the soft earth on either side of the lawn. And no side entrance.

The impossible does not happen. Absurd not to have thought of it sooner. Her row of little houses must have been built some time in the eighteenth century as working men's cottages, to service the big houses on the other side of the High Street. Their gardens, she knew, ran uphill behind them into open country, except where patches had been sold off for development. So where had their stables been? Obviously, across the mews lane at the bottom of her garden.

She fetched the secateurs and advanced on the rampant polygonum there. When you really looked, it was obvious enough. Someone had indeed forced their way through here, she saw as she cut savagely at the tough stems. It must have been a very small person, though, probably just a neighbouring child, who had found the way and made the secret garden their own. And here was the door, solidly set in the back wall, badly needing paint, and – she turned the handle – unlocked.

What a fright about nothing. Standing in the deserted

lane, she looked at the graveyard wall facing her and saw that it was comparatively new, late nineteenth or even early twentieth century brick. The stables must have been pulled down at some point and the graveyard extended, probably when the advent of the motor car began to make horses redundant. Looking up and down the quiet lane she saw that most of the other back entrances had been bricked up. No need to do that herself; her own door seemed solid enough behind its screen of polygonum; but she would go down to the ironmonger who actually existed in the pedestrian precinct by the station and buy herself a large bolt. She even felt a little sorry for the unknown child, who had made her garden its own and would now find itself locked out. They had done no damage, after all, left no litter, lit no fires. But she did not want them watching her through her kitchen window.

She bought the bolt that afternoon and screwed it on herself, thinking with amusement that back at the Hall she would have had to wait for Barnes, the chauffeur, to get around to doing such a job for her. Inevitably it reminded her of one of the arguments she had had with Geoffrey. She had very much wanted to get Barnes to teach her to drive, but Geoffrey had been set against it. 'Much more dignified to let Barnes drive you,' he had insisted.

Who wants to be dignified? But, as so often, she had not said it. Perhaps she would take lessons now. Perhaps not. All her principles were against it. She had bought this house, after all, and moved into Leyning so that she would be able to get about by public transport, such as it was. By taking the short cut across the graveyard she could be at the station in ten minutes. Less, now, she thought, if she used her back gate. She must have a proper lock put on, next time she had someone working about the place, so she could go out that way and leave all safe behind her.

The telephone rang again a couple of times that night, and she remembered that she had never got in touch with the operator. The second time, instead of a click when the receiver was replaced at the other end there was the sound of slightly asthmatic breathing. She did not like it at all.

The operator, when she called next morning, was friendly, but not very helpful, making it clear that two days' worth of odd calls on a new line were not much to complain about. It's like someone having to get killed before you get a pedestrian crossing, Patience thought, replacing the receiver. The front door bell rang. She hurried to answer it, half expecting to find nobody there, stood for a minute, looking the strange woman up and down. Not a strange woman.

"Hullo, Patience," said Mary Brigance. What was her surname now? "You never answer my letters, so I thought I'd take the bull by the horns and come and see you. Are you going to ask me in?"

For a moment, Patience hesitated. She had meant the break to be absolute, and to stay that way. But after all that time? And all that had happened? Besides, those same two Conservative ladies were hovering on the other side of the road, quite obviously watching. She swung the heavy door wider. "I suppose I am," she said, and knew it sounded ungracious.

"Good." Mary stripped off leather driving gloves and dropped them on the chest by the door. "Mark said I had to get in, even if it meant forcing an entrance."

"Mark?" She had thought she would never say that name

again. Moving mechanically while her heart raced, she took Mary's jacket.

"He writes to me sometimes." Mary was just as elegant and almost as beautiful as ever, rakishly thin with a crop of startling silver hair. "When he can. He'd been reading through back files of *The Times*, saw something about you. Gossipy rags they are these days; fancy hashing up all that old story. I don't suppose you liked it much."

"I didn't see it."

"Strong-minded. It was the first Mark had heard of Geoffrey Crankshaw's death. Should I condole?' she enquired with a quick, bright glance.

"No, thanks." They seemed to have moved into the kitchen and Patience reached for the kettle. "Coffee?"

"I'd rather have a drink." Mary looked at the wall clock. "Less trouble and more fun. And then I'm taking you out to lunch. I saw a friendly-looking pub a mile or so out of town. Sunshine in the garden, too. We could have a sandwich and tell each other the stories of our lives without your nosy neighbours listening in."

"Nosy neighbours?"

"You must have noticed the two old things across the road. And there was someone lurking around on the pavement outside when I first drove by looking for somewhere to park. A teenager by the look of it, and up to no good, I thought. Maybe you should have moved further . . . Thanks. I'm glad to see you still like it dry." She took the glass of sherry Patience had poured.

"It's all I've got, I'm afraid. Not really your line, Mary." She was surprised to hear the Christian name come out so easily.

133

"Oh, I'm a reformed character. Have been for years. My husband before last was teetotal, God help me."

"And the present one?"

"Past. I've just left him."

"Oh?" They had settled on either side of the dining table and Patience looked at her questioningly.

"'Oh' it is. He turned out to be an alcoholic with a tendency to violence. Looking back I sometimes wish I'd hung on to poor Tony Wetherall."

"What happened to him?"

"He's all right. He married a very suitable girl and they have at least five children. I'm godma to one of them, I rather think." She sipped her sherry. "You never gave us a chance to thank you for that money, Patience, which was more than we deserved, I reckon. And sometimes I wonder if I mightn't have been better without it. Looking back, I suspect I liked my job – when I had it – better than any of my husbands."

"Any children?"

"No, alas. Tony didn't want them, and with the others they just didn't happen. Too bad; I'd have liked them."

"Oh, so would I." But that was something about which she absolutely would not talk. "It's really good to see you, Mary." It was.

"Isn't it? I thought I'd be able to talk to you, and you've not really changed a bit, Patience, not now you've got that frozen look off your face. Do you know, when you opened the door, you looked, just for a minute, that way you did when you came into the study, back at the Hall, and found us all there, conniving against you. And I don't blame you for a moment. But, honest and true, Patience, Mark and I were going to break ranks if the inquest had gone the other way. You must – *please* – believe that."

"I'd like to." The old wound was bleeding again.

"So, come out to lunch and let's talk. I rather need a family ear."

"No, let's stay here. You'll be my first guest. Frozen pizza and salad, but I brought away all Geoffrey's wine hoard, and the cheese is good."

"Lovely. But don't let me drink too much. And ply me with coffee afterwards. I'm on my way to the ferry."

"Newhaven?"

"Yes, if they don't cancel it. I'm going to meet Mark; he's got some leave."

"Leave? What from? He's not retired?" As she spoke she plunged into the deep freeze and extricated the pizza from under several bags of frozen vegetables.

"Lord, no. Something very hush-hush all over the world. They wouldn't let him go. Said they couldn't spare him. You don't know anything about any of us, do you, Patience?"

"No. I didn't want to." It sounded as bleak as she had felt.

"I shall tell you, just the same. We're your family, after all. When you come right down to it, all you've got. Except those friends of yours – what was their name, Cunningham?"

"That's it. They live in the south of France now. I went to see them last summer."

"And it didn't work?" Mary had always been quick. She raised her glass: "Here's to the gloomy catalogue. Mother and Uncle Joseph are both dead; Emily is in a home and so is Seward – senile he is – and Grisel has taken on a new lease

135

of life. I rather think she had him sectioned, or whatever they call it these days. She certainly made it crystal clear she didn't mean to look after him any more and got away with it."

"What about Ludwig and Leonora?" It was strange to find herself interested again, after all these years, in the family that had nearly got her hanged.

"Do you know, they vanished. Into the U S of A, I rather think, from something Grisel said once, but not a whisper, not a Christmas card, certainly not a wedding announcement."

"And not much loss," said Patience.

"You mean you liked them even less than you did the rest of us? Well, I suppose that's good news of a kind. You've not asked about Priss."

"I'd forgotten all about her."

"One does tend to, but she was the great surprise. She married Paul Protheroe."

"What?"

"I said it would surprise you. It turned out they'd been carrying on all the time. Very much unbeknownst to old Gran. No wonder Priss had so little use for those spineless young men her mother dragged down for her."

"Priss and Paul Protheroe!" Ideas were jangling against each other in Patience's mind. One thing she and Geoffrey had agreed on was their conviction that her cousin Paul had contrived to embezzle her money during her long minority, but there had been no way of proving it. "That is a surprise."

"And you'd be surprised, too, if you saw Priss. She made herself over when she got away from the Hall; and to some purpose."

"Dark hair," said Patience out of deep instinct.

"You're quite right; suits her much better than that mouse colour. Though mind you, she's kept it that way a bit too long."

"Children?"

The telephone rang.

"Hell," said Patience. She picked it up and got no answer. "I'm being harassed," she told Mary. "It's a dead bore; I'll tell you about it." She was really glad now that Mary had come. "But if you are going to catch the ferry we ought to be thinking about lunch. I'll fetch us up some wine. Red or white?"

"Oh, red, don't you think, now it's so good for our hearts. Don't tell me you have a cellar?"

"Yes; a huge one. It's got the boiler in, but there's a cool corner at the other end for the wine. It's got a TudorBethan bread oven in. Come and see."

"You love this house, don't you?"

"Yes. Love at first sight."

"I don't blame you. It's friendly somehow. Not like the Hall."

"You felt that too?"

"Oh, yes." She followed Patience into the front hall where a bolted door opened on to steep steps, a musty smell and the sound of the boiler muttering contentedly to itself.

"Careful on the steps." Patience switched on an overhead light, started down and gave something between a gasp and a scream. "What on earth—"

Craning over her shoulder, Mary too saw the crimson pool gleaming in the light from the naked bulb. "Dear God! What's happened?"

"I don't know." They both looked nervously into the dark corners of the cellar where the light did not reach. "I'll get a flashlight." Her voice shook. She reached to take Mary's hand. "I'm so glad you're here, Mary."

"Yes." They moved back, silent, in single file up the narrow stair.

"It must be recent, to look like that." Neither of them had said the word 'blood'. Patience picked her heavy duty flashlight out of the hall cupboard and led the way back down. "Oh!" As she flashed the torch on to the sinister pool they both saw that it was not blood at all. "Paint!"

"But still wet," said Mary. "How on earth?"

"It's under the area opening." Patience had begun to think. She flashed the torch upwards. "See. The gas board made me put a grille in for air for the boiler. Someone must have poured it down."

"What a disgusting trick," said Mary. "It's not like you to have enemies, Patience."

"That's what I'd have thought," said Patience, plucking a random bottle of red wine from the rack. "Let's get out of here. I'll clear it up tomorrow. It'll take gallons of turps."

"But at least it won't do any harm down there," said Mary. "Just a very nasty prank. And, come to think, I did see that teenager loitering when I drove by. I told you I thought she was up to no good."

"She?"

"Oh, definitely – hippie type; trailing skirts; are there gypsies in town?"

"Not that I know of." Patience had automatically uncorked the bottle and poured wine for them both. "I smell pizza; let's eat. It will make us feel better."

"There's room." Mary took the plate Patience passed her. "I think you should tell the police."

"No!" Patience took a gulp of wine. "Not the police, Mary. I know it's not reasonable, but I can't help it. After those nights in that cell I don't care if I never see the police again. You just don't know what it's like to be treated as worthless, assumed guilty. I'd rather die than go to them."

"Oh, Patience!" Mary reached out a hand to take hers. "I am so sorry." And then: "You might have died down there in your cellar, you know. On your own, you might have fallen, knocked yourself out. Who would have known you were there?"

"No one." They faced it together, soberly, eating pizza without tasting it.

Eight

"I hate to go." Mary looked at the clock and finished her coffee. "If only there was a way I could get in touch with Mark."

"But there isn't." They had been through this already. "I'll be all right, Mary, I truly will."

"And you do promise to go to the police if anything else happens?"

"Yes, cross my heart and hope to die." They smiled at each other, remembering childhood, and Mary reached out impulsively to kiss Patience on the cheek. "I'm so glad I came," she said. "I'll ring the minute I get back. Your love to Mark?"

"Why not?" The quick kiss had stirred something in Patience. "Drive carefully."

"I do."

"Well, that's a change. Oh, I do thank you for coming, Mary. It's been too long."

"Soon again." She was off, walking briskly down the street towards her car, and Patience shut the door behind her and faced her house, which felt empty for the first time. She rather wished there was something to be done in the kitchen, but Mary had insisted on washing up. Instead, she would go down to the ironmonger and buy white spirit to clean up that sinister pool of blood red paint. The house would feel better after that. Making light to Mary about the intruder in her garden, she had almost convinced herself that this act of vandalism had been merely a childish revenge for the bolted garden door. But, "Not a very nice child," Mary had said.

The white spirit and the scraper that the friendly ironmonger sold her were heavier than Patience had expected. The light was beginning to fade by the time she started home and she paused at the wicket gate that led into the graveyard. The path across it was both quicker and prettier than the main road and the gates were never locked until full dark. Idiotic to blench at taking it. She pushed open the gate and started up the gently sloping path between ancient gravestones. She usually paused to notice a name here, an odd epitaph there, but today she found herself instinctively hurrying.

She paused at last, breathless, to look back at the view of the river. Turning, she was aware of flurried movement. Someone was there, too close behind her, unheard because of traffic noise. A child? A woman? One arm raised. Patience reached out her own free hand and grabbed it.

"Flour!" she exclaimed as the open bag fell and burst on the ground. "What a disgusting trick!" Amazing to find herself instinctively remembering the defence techniques she had learned at college all those years ago. "Don't try to get away," she told the savagely writhing figure. "Or I'll really hurt you. That's better." Her captive had stopped struggling and was still, swearing under her breath. She

141

smelled, Patience noticed with distaste. "Not a child," she said. "So, no excuses."

"Look who's talking." The voice was a surprise: Queen's English with a slight west country burr and the faintest hint of an asthmatic wheeze. "What excuse is there for you, Mrs bloody Crankshaw?"

"What do you mean?" She used her strong grip to pull her opponent nearer to the light at the top of the graveyard, and saw that despite her foul language she was not much more than a child, skeleton thin, a gypsy-like creature in the trailing skirts Mary had described.

"You killed my mother!" It was spat at her rather than spoken.

"I beg your pardon!" Patience put the ironmonger's heavy bag down on the bench by the graveyard gate and pulled the girl round to face her. She did not think she was drugged; perhaps she was mad. It seemed the only explanation. "I've never seen you in my life before and I've no more idea who your mother is than the man in the moon."

"Not is. Was. I told you, you killed her." Another stream of curses followed.

"And I tell you that's nonsense." Soon, now, the man would come to lock the gate. "You may know me but I most certainly don't know you."

"Oh yes you do. I'm Veronica."

"I'm none the wiser. Veronica who?"

"Crankshaw, it should be!"

"What? I don't understand." But was she beginning to?

"Oh yes you bloody do. You're just pretending. You knew all the time and didn't give a damn. Dad always said you were a selfish cow."

"Dad?" Her grip tightened on the thin wrist.

"Your handsome husband. My fine father. The man who would be Prime Minister if he could only get into Parliament. I really believed it all when I was a kid. All that talk. Mustn't say a word; mustn't do a thing to spoil his precious career. But he'd look after us; no need to worry; everything under control – safe as houses—"

She was working up towards hysteria when a man's voice interrupted. "Excuse me, ma'am, closing time."

"Oh, yes, thank you." Patience, mentally reeling, took an instant decision. She let go of the hand she had held so tight. "You'd better come home with me," she said. "When did you last eat?"

"Home? To your house?" But she had not turned to run.

"Well, yes. Better than sleeping rough, surely? And it does seem as if we have something to talk about, you and I." She picked up the ironmonger's bag. "You must believe that I knew nothing about you." Her eyes met defiant grey ones.

"I almost do." They had left the graveyard now and were walking down the lane, side by side, presenting a picture of amity to the puzzled groundsman. "I've been watching you."

"I know," said Patience quietly. "And telephoning."

"Yes. You're not like he said. Not at all."

"I don't suppose I am. But at least you knew about me!" She had been living with more lies than she had imagined and it was amazing how it hurt. Questions seethed in her mind, but not yet.

"Only because Mum saw his picture in the paper. With you. At a dinner. Mr and Mrs. She was a loving fool, was Mum, but not such a fool he could lie his way out of that."

"Oh dear," said Patience inadequately. "Here, take this bag while I find my key. You won't bash me with it, will you?"

"No, honest to God I won't. I should have had more sense than to believe him. No brighter than poor Mum after all." They were in the hall now, and she looked about her with quick, nervous glances. "This is the bit I couldn't see. I like your house. That's when I began to wonder a bit. About you. But by then I couldn't stop. It was being so angry kept me going."

"You found the back door in the wall." It was hardly a question.

"I figured there had to be one. I've been sleeping in the shed. I've done no damage. Not yet." It hung ominously in the air between them.

Except for a little matter of red paint in the cellar. But the girl was shivering. With cold, with shock – with fright? And now that Patience could see her, there was no mistaking the likeness to Geoffrey Crankshaw. "You're my stepdaughter," she said slowly, taking it in. "How very strange. Which would you like first, Veronica, a meal or a bath?"

"Oh, a bath, please!" It broke the last bastion of resistance and she dissolved into tears.

She was frighteningly thin inside the drooping clothes, and Patience, silently considering her own neat, elderly wardrobe, remembered a light wool caftan she had seldom worn. Handing this to her surprise guest along with a new pair of Marks and Spencer knickers, she showed her to the bathroom and turned on the taps. "My bra would be far too big, but I don't suppose you need one. Lots of bath stuff; don't hurry; I'll be making soup. Oh, dump your things outside the door and I'll put them in the machine. Bit of luck they'll be dry by morning. You'll be all right? Don't lock the door, just in case. Oh—" She hesitated in the doorway. "You're not a vegetarian or anything, are you?"

"No." It got her an attempt at a laugh. "Do I look like one? It's this gear I borrowed, I reckon." And then, with difficulty: "Thanks."

Slicing onions for soup, Patience made herself concentrate on the matter in hand: stock from the deep freeze, vegetables, a potato to thicken it. When it was simmering on the back burner she went quietly upstairs to put a hot pad in the spare room bed, glad that she had decided to make one up, just in case. Then back down to set the table with wholemeal bread, cold tongue from a tin, cheese and fruit, dressing for a salad. Best not give the child wine. How old was she? As she worked, the questions battered at her mind. Her whole past had turned upside down. Geoffrey had never wanted children, afraid that they would interfere with his career. It was one of the many things she had not learned about him until too late. Much too late. Her child would have been in its forties now. His forties? Her forties?

Her hand shook as she poured the soup into the blender. When it was safely back on the stove to simmer she went out into the hall to listen and was glad to hear the bathroom door open. "Supper's ready when you are," she called up the stairs. "But don't hurry; it'll keep."

"I can't wait! I can smell it. It's killing me." Veronica had washed her hair and it clung pale and damp around the face that was so like Geoffrey's. Grey eyes met Patience's. "I don't know what to say."

"Then don't try." Patience was pouring soup into bowls. "And don't eat too fast; it might make you sick."

"Not this, it wouldn't." But she paused to take the bread Patience passed her and crumble it into the thick soup. "It's ace," she said after a few more mouthfuls. "You didn't buy this from Tesco."

"No, I made it. Have some more."

"Please." She passed over her empty bowl, and they ate for a while in silence, Patience battening down the questions until the time was right.

"I've been off my head." Veronica put down her spoon and looked across the table. "Round the bend. Nuts. Like it all happened so fast, when Mum got ill. After he died. Then the money stopped coming." Her words were beginning to slur.

"If you've been trying to sleep in that shed you must be dead on your feet," Patience told her. "That's probably enough to eat for now, and bed's what you need. Come along, Veronica, things will look better in the morning."

"You're not going to throw me out? Call the cops?"

"Good God, no. What an idea! Come along now, your bed's all ready." She had to help Veronica to her feet and up the stairs, and wondered whether she should send for the doctor. But every instinct was against it. Young Dr Findlayson, like his father before him, was a very important link in the friendly chain of gossip that held Leyning together. Before he saw Veronica Crankshaw, they must have their story ready for him. "Sleep as long as you can." She smiled from the doorway. "We'll talk in the morning."

The doorbell rang while Patience was finishing the supper

dishes. Well, this time there was likely to be someone there, and she had a pretty good idea who it would be. She took off her apron and made her leisurely way to the door. She was right. It was Mrs Vansittart, who lived across the road.

"Oh, what a relief," she said at the sight of Patience. "Forgive the intrusion, my dear, but to tell you the truth I was a little anxious about you. I happened to see you come back earlier on with a very odd-looking young person I'd seen hanging around. I really thought I ought to come and make sure you were all right."

"How very kind of you, Mrs Vansittart. And brave too, in the dark. I'm really grateful. But it's quite all right, thank you. It's a young friend of mine who has been having a bit of a bad time. Her mother died suddenly, and she seems to have gone off the rails a bit. I am so glad I ran into her; she's resting now. I expect I'll hear all about it when she feels better. Boyfriend problems, too, I imagine. You know how they are, the young."

"Oh dear me, yes. Always in one kind of trouble or other. How nice you have made the little house." She was peering brightly round the hall. "Do you still have the drawing room upstairs?"

"Yes, but I'm afraid I mustn't take you up to see it tonight. I've just got Veronica off to bed and I don't want to disturb her."

"Veronica. What a pretty name. And you are washing her clothes for her!" The machine had just gone into a new cycle. "Such a good hostess. I'm so very glad to find it is all for the best, my dear. You must come and see me very soon and tell me all about the poor young thing. Or bring her?"

"How very kind of you." Patience had learned over the

years the technique of the gentle irrevocable movement towards the front door. "It was really good of you to come." She meant it. It might have been inquisitive of the old lady, but it had also been brave.

It was still only nine o'clock when the washing machine fell silent and Patience could hang the sad clothes on the airer in the utility room. There was no warmth in the shabby cotton skirt and shirt and the long grey cardigan was not much better. How in the world had Veronica managed to sleep at all in the shed? And how long had she been camping there? On the thought, she took a flashlight and went down the garden to look for signs of the secret occupation, half afraid of the sordid, smelly scene she might find.

Nothing of the sort. The poor child must have been going clear down to the public loos at the station . . . How odd to be thinking of the unknown menace who had haunted her as a poor child. But that was clearly what she was. "Go very carefully," Patience warned herself, wishing she had more experience of the young.

She stood for a moment, looking up at the stars, finding her garden friendly again, the unknown threat gone. But inevitably her thoughts moved on to Geoffrey and what she had learned about him. He had deceived her, basically, consistently and successfully. For how long?

Did it matter? It was her mistake that she had stayed with him, without love, all those years. What a waste, she thought, what a terrible waste, and decided to stop dredging in the useless past and go to bed. Tomorrow there would be things to do, decisions to make.

She picked a couple of bananas from the fruit bowl and left them on the small table outside the spare room door in case her guest should wake hungry in the night. Then she put herself to bed with the poems of U. A. Fanthorpe and soon fell asleep, braced, somehow, and comforted.

In the morning the bananas had gone and there was no sound of life from the spare room. She went quietly downstairs, put on the kettle, got croissants out of the deep freeze, and fixed a grapefruit. Her own breakfast finished, she was sitting with her elbows on the table drinking coffee and reading the *Independent* when she heard movement from above. "Good morning! Could you eat a boiled egg?" she called up the stairs. "Your clothes aren't quite dry yet, I'm afraid. Can you bear the caftan again for the time being?"

"Sure. An egg would be super." Veronica appeared at the top of the stairs, tousle-headed in the pyjamas Patience had lent her. "Thanks a million for the bananas. They saved my life. Like you!" She turned crimson and dived back into her room.

She had a little colour this morning, Patience saw with pleasure when she joined her. "I hope you slept well. Eat your grapefruit while I boil your egg." She had promised herself not to ask a single question until breakfast was over.

Veronica was eyeing the cafetière. "Cool," she said. "Real coffee like Mum made."

"Do you want to talk about her?" Breaking her resolve already, Patience poured and passed her guest a cup of coffee as she started on the grapefruit.

"I think so." She sipped coffee and smiled for the first time across the cup at Patience. "Super coffee." And then, "What's the matter?"

"You're so like your father . . ." The smile had all Geoffrey's dangerous charm.

149

"I know. I'm sorry." She meant it. "Maybe if it hadn't been for that I'd have bitten the bullet and gone to Mum's people when she got ill. But she said no, over her dead body we went to them. And that's what it came down to." Her eyes met Patience's, full of tears. "Then, it went so fast, once I made them take her into hospital—"

"Made?"

"The doctor kept talking about a virus . . . Like, he'd never seen Mum, didn't know her, she didn't get ill – that's why I knew it was bad when she just stayed in bed, but you couldn't tell him. He wouldn't listen – well, he was busy, of course."

"They all are," said Patience, silently passing egg and toast and refilling her cup.

"Yes. So I went into the surgery and made a scene." Patience could imagine it. "And then he came, and took her in, and scanned her, and she just curled up and died."

"I'm sorry."

"Don't be. Not for her. I think, like, she was glad to go, even if it hadn't been for the pain. And they were super in the hospital, once they knew. Couldn't have been kinder. To me too. But not much they could do afterwards. We didn't have any friends, you see, Mum and I. She was always waiting around for him to come; didn't want arrangements that got in the way. And we couldn't talk about him; if you're in a lie all the time you can't have friends . . . What is it?"

"It's what he did to me too," Patience said. "So, did you get in touch with her family after she died? Get them to help you?"

"No way! If she hadn't wanted them alive, I wasn't going to have them come shoving in when she was gone. Besides,

I was the problem, wasn't I? Once she was gone they weren't likely to be keen on the family bastard, were they? Coming crawling for help? No, thanks! The social services helped me, and the lawyer was kind, in his way, and I said my goodbyes alone, on a wet Thursday at the crematorium, with no flowers. And, like, all the time, I was getting angrier and angrier with you, making it all your fault we'd got into that mess. If you'd only divorced him he'd have married her; it would all have been different. But as you wouldn't—"

"Wouldn't?" Patience interrupted her. "Veronica, he never asked me to. I knew nothing. I only wish I had."

"I see that now. I think I began to wonder when I got here, started watching you, saw what you were like. You weren't a bit like he said." She took a breath. "Poor Mum, she should have spotted it. From the picture in the paper. I found it after she died. She'd kept it. You were pretty when you were young, weren't you? Bright-looking, neat. Not a fat slob with more money than was good for her." Her imitation of her father's voice sent a shiver down Patience's spine.

"Horrible." She looked back down the long range of wasted years she had lived with Veronica's treacherous father. "How old are you?"

"Eighteen." She took a steadying sip of coffee, aware, Patience thought, of what she was really being asked. "But it had been going on for years before me. Him and Mum. Like, I wrecked it for her. A menopause mistake. No way he wanted me. Told Mum to get rid of me. But she wouldn't. She told me that and I believe her."

"I'm sure you are right to." A better woman than me, thought Patience.

"He kept away for a while, Mum said; gave her a bit more

151

money and kept away. He never did like me. Didn't pretend to. But then" – a flicker of a smile – "I hated him right back. Mum used to leave me with the neighbours mostly. When he came. She was quite different then, everything about her. I hated that too."

"She must have loved him very much," said Patience.

"Oh, she did. I see that now. That's why she stood for it. Couldn't help herself. Like, he was her life. And I spoiled it for her. She talked a bit, rambling, when she was dying. They let me sit with her all the time. Super, they were. I think there must have been a point when she really thought he was going to get rid of you . . . Sorry!" A quick, apologetic glance. "Marry her; adopt me. Then he saw me one time and saw how like him I looked. I'd have been a dead giveaway. And that was that. I reckon that was when the cancer started, but she never said a thing. Just let it go. I suppose she wanted to die, really."

"Hard on you."

"All my fault."

"No, Veronica. All his. How did they meet?" And then: "Sorry. Do you mind talking about it?"

"Let's get it over with. I can see you need to know the lot. It was way back, Suez time, Mum said. Some political do in Plymouth and he was speaking. Freemasons, or something. Mum's dad was chair, like, and he took her along to the dinner after because her mother wasn't well. It was love at first sight, Mum said. Both of them. No question. She was only seventeen. Younger than I am. He stayed on for a few days after the meeting. To be with her. You remember?" She had seen something in Patience's face.

"Yes, I remember. He rang to say he thought there was a

chance of the seat there. He'd stay a bit and go for it. We'd been married five years then." She swallowed. She owed the truth in exchange. "I was well and truly out of love with him by then, if I'd ever been in. Knew it had all been an appalling mistake. I'll tell you about it some time. Perhaps. But I was sure he still loved me. Needed me. My mistake. So it had gone on for years before you were born?"

"Yes. She lived for him, waited for him; he fouled up everything for her. She didn't talk about it much. She always tried so hard to find excuses. But that's what it came down to. For a while she did all the usual things. Left school, you know, did a cordon bleu cookery course, shared a flat with two other girls. And had offers of course."

"And turned them down?"

"And turned them down. From what she said, I think he always managed to turn up just in time, when she was beginning to get interested in someone else. And that was that. I'm sorry." She looked across the table at Patience. "Should I be telling you this?"

"Of course you should. I was just thinking about all the times he said he had urgent, sudden political business. And vanished. We didn't talk politics much, after Suez," she explained, and saw that it did not mean anything to Veronica. "I should have guessed," she said sadly. "Found out. Done something."

"Christ, don't you start blaming yourself too! That's what Mum always did. Said it was all her fault. Bloody nonsense."

"Maybe," said Patience, "But easier that way, somehow. You see, Veronica, you must understand: I was glad when he went away. I was happier without him."

153

"And you never did anything about it? But that's gruesome."

"I know. I'm ashamed. I've only lived half a life, and it's been my own fault."

"Oh, fuck 'fault'!" said Veronica. And then: "Sorry! I'll try not to." She giggled. "You looked just like Mother Serena," she said. "At the convent . . . Mum sent me to her old school to get me out of the way," she explained. "He was glad to pay for that." Something about Patience's silence alerted her. "Was it your money – you paying? All the time? Didn't you notice?"

"No. I'm ashamed of that too. But I never thought not to trust him, you see."

"A mistake."

"Yes. So, you're a Catholic?"

"Was. School cured me of that. And the way Mum's parents behaved to her. Not much bloody Christianity about that. Oh, sorry, I will try not to. What shall I say? 'Basingstoke'?"

"Or 'By our Lady'," Patience suggested. She looked at the kitchen clock. "We're wasting time. We've got to get a story together before the neighbours start calling to make sure you haven't mugged me in the night."

"What?"

"You must have lived in a small town at some point?"

"Yes. St Ives. I grew up there. Mum modelled a bit."

"Well, then, you know how news travels. My neighbour across the road saw us come back last night. She sits in her front window. She dropped in after you'd gone to bed to make sure I was OK. Nice of her really. I said you were a young friend, in trouble. She'll be back."

"Course she will. True enough about the trouble, but decent of you to say 'friend'."

"More than that, I hope." Her mind had been racing, behind the scenes of this extraordinary conversation, and now she found that it had made itself up. "You are going to stay with me, aren't you, Veronica? Let me look after you? The only thing that I keep wondering is how many people are going to notice just how like Geoffrey you look. Because everyone knows him in Leyning, of course. So who in the world are we going to say you are?"

"I don't understand." She picked up a cold croissant and nibbled it absent-mindedly, dropping crumbs on the table, her eyes fixed on Patience. Asking something?

"Well, I can't exactly say, 'This is a daughter I didn't know I had', can I, though I'd like to." She reached across the table to grasp Veronica's hand. "You are going to let me adopt you, Veronica?"

"What?" She put down her coffee cup, stared across the table. "You're raving—"

"I'm not, you know." Patience swallowed a lump in her throat. "I don't believe in God, worse luck, but if I did, I'd think I was being given a second chance. I'm going to tell you something I've never told a soul. I started a baby, quite early on, with Geoffrey. Oh, I still remember how pleased I was. Until I told him. He made me get rid of it."

"And you did?"

"Yes. Your mother was a better woman than I am. I've never forgiven myself. Or him. It was the end of the marriage, really, so far as I was concerned. I hated him touching me after that, but he never noticed. He wasn't a noticing man. What I'm saying, Veronica, is that there was

155

nothing of him for your mother to take away from me. I'd lost him already. And the baby."

"But for Christ's sake, why didn't you leave him?"

"You may well ask. But, remember, it wasn't so easy then. And I still believed in his career – just as your mother did. He was a very convincing man. Back when it happened, long before Suez, I really thought he was going to do some good in the world. It was my job to back him. It's a long story, Veronica, and I'll probably tell it you one day, but I did owe him a great deal. And I truly thought he needed me. If he'd only told me about your mother, and you, I'd have divorced him like a shot. I'd even have let him divorce me. So, you see, it's all my fault . . . No, please don't say it! I hate that word."

"Right," said Veronica. "But just the same, let's not fool around wondering whose fault it all is. Except his. I say, what am I going to call you?"

"Oh, Patience, please. I'm not mad about the rest of it. And you? You said you should be Crankshaw?"

"He wouldn't let Mum name him as father. So I've her name, Lavolle, but of course it made her people madder at her than ever. That's why she moved to St Ives in the end, to get clear the other side of the county from them. It was better there, she said, right from the start. She'd got away from the county grapevine and was just Mrs Lavolle with a baby and no husband. And she was lovely, Mum; all the artist crowd there liked to use her as a model, and they let her bring me along. There's a picture of me in the Tate there only you wouldn't recognise me, of course, it being an abstract."

"So you went to school there?"

"Primary school, yes. I loved it. Friends all over town,

walking to school together, going home to tea, even spending the night, times Mum wanted to get rid of me. It was when I started to grow up and wise up that she packed me off to the nuns. They thought it was their Christian duty to have me, see, and, boy, did they let me know it. And my clothes were all wrong – charity shops! – and I didn't go skiing at Christmas . . . I'd have run away if there'd been anywhere to run to. It's not nice, knowing your mum doesn't want you at home. But I stuck it out and got my GCSEs. Like, I'm not stupid, though I wouldn't blame you for thinking so; and then he died, and Mum got ill, and I just dropped out. Fair's fair: the nuns did write and offer me a schol after Mum died and the money stopped coming. I'd have laughed if I hadn't been crying. They wanted my A level results, see, for their bloody league tables."

"So you're not stupid. Well, we'll just have to arrange for you to take the As here next year."

Veronica put down her cup. "You really mean it?"

"Of course I mean it. I've never been so sure of anything in my life. So, the first thing is to arrange to collect your things."

"Things? I've got no things."

"What do you mean?"

"It was a council flat, see; Mum was the tenant. When she died, I didn't seem to exist. And then there was one of those muddles; you know the social." She gave a disconcerting smile. "Well, no, I suppose you don't. But muddles they're good at. I went to stay with friends after the funeral and got back to find they'd cleared the flat. It had all gone to the tip. And that was that. All I had was the shoulder bag I'd taken with me, make-up and bits." She blushed, and looked about twelve. "It's stashed away at the back of your shed. My worldly possessions."

"Well, you'd better go and get them," said Patience. "And then let's go to Brighton, and buy you some clothes."

Nine

"Gruesome." Veronica was looking with distaste at her dry clothes. "Must I wear them? They're not mine! It was a squat, see, where my friend lived. I felt such a fool in my funeral blacks one of the girls lent me these. They were OK there, but there's no way they are here. I bet you've got leggings and a shirt I could wear. I loathe these drippy skirts. Actually, I thought afterwards that the social might have been more help if I'd looked different. You know what I mean? But I wasn't caring, then. Nor thinking, much. It was all gone, see: my past, my pictures of Mum, everything."

"Oh, Veronica!" Patience was not quite sure how it happened but found that she had the thin, shaking body in her arms and Veronica crying her heart out on her shoulder.

She cried a little too, and then, presently, said, "Do you know, you're absolutely right. I have got a pair of leggings tucked away somewhere. I bought them for yoga once, and then lost my nerve. And it doesn't matter how big a shirt is, does it? Let's go and have a look."

There is something very friendly about going through a wardrobe together. Having recently unpacked them, Patience put her hand on the black leggings at once, and Veronica, riffling through the clothes in the built-in cupboard, came up

159

with a dark blue corduroy shirt and a devastating comment: "You dress to be invisible. Why?"

"Goodness." Looking over her shoulder at the neat row of greys and browns and muted blues, Patience saw just what she meant. "I suppose that's what I want."

"Nutty. Tell you what, I'll make a deal with you. You can dress me if you'll let me dress you. It's what I mean to do, see. Not so much fashion design as fashion advice. I'd love to get my hands on you. If you can really afford it? I reckon you must be able to, if my foul father could have rooked you of all that money and you never even noticed."

"You're absolutely right," Patience said ruefully. "I feel such a fool."

"It's not foolish to trust people." Veronica pulled on the leggings, unzipped the caftan and shrugged into the blue shirt. "Transformation scene. And a lesson for you in what clothes can do."

"You could be a model. Fashion, not artist's." Patience was admiring the striking, long-legged figure in the mirror. "You've the twiggy build for one."

"I know. Too thin by half. Mum used to moan about it. But that's how I reckoned to keep myself while I got started, only I didn't know anyone to get me into the fashion scene. That's what counts. And I bet you don't either."

"I'm afraid not." Patience was beginning to hope that all was going to be very well. "But we've a year to think about that, while you get those A levels."

"Must I?"

"You know you must. You're not a fool, Veronica, you said so yourself. Pretty soon, the way things are going, you'll need three As to be a milkman. There's nowhere here in Leyning

160

but the comprehensive; I think it will have to be Lewes or Brighton. Sixth form college? Tech, maybe? You could do it by train. I don't suppose you drive?"

"Not officially. No car, no test. But, look, we're going so fast. Are you sure you're really, really serious? We won't wake up tomorrow and find it was all a crazy dream?"

"I shan't." Patience looked at her watch. "If we hurry we can catch the eleven ten to Brighton. We'll get some lunch there."

"Super," said Veronica.

They began in Marks and Spencer, where Veronica swiftly and efficiently chose and tried on two pairs of jeans, three shirts and what she laughingly called a 'whole trousseau' of underwear. With these in her arms, she plucked a deep crimson blouse from a rack. "And this for you," she said.

"But I don't wear red. And I'm not dressed for trying on."

"No need with this. It'll fit. And you ought to wear red. I won't have these if you won't have that."

"Blackmail." But Patience was glad to produce her charge card and pay for the lot. "Now let's see how they are getting on with the new shopping centre," she said, leading the way across the road.

"I never liked them much. Full of everything you don't want, and no air to breathe. Look at the ladders! It really isn't open yet, you know, and I hate to say it but I'm hungry again. All that trying on! But you have to, with jeans. I bet there's a pub round here somewhere would give us a good, thick sandwich."

"But I hate the push and shove at the bar. I really am invisible there. I thought of a restaurant in the Lanes somewhere."

"And spend a fortune to take hours? Honestly, I'd rather

have time for a look at the sea. I miss it, you know. It's all around you in St Ives. And then we've got to find you something to wear with that shirt. Black pants, I think. Not M and S. Not for you."

"But I don't wear trousers."

"Well, you ought to. But we'll get you a skirt, too, if you like. Where do you usually shop?"

"Jaeger's and Hannington's. It's the old established department store here," she explained. "And I like it. They still treat you like a person."

"Right, we'll go there after lunch. Here's our pub." She pushed open the door, led the way in and settled Patience firmly at a table for two. "You mind the shopping, Patience, while I get us a menu."

"And a drink," said Patience, whose heart leapt every time Veronica used her name. "Shandy for me." She found a twenty pound note in her purse and handed it over.

Looking across the table at Veronica sipping orange juice while they waited for their cheese baguettes, Patience spoke from her heart. "I feel like the old woman in the nursery rhyme," she said. "You know the one: 'Lawks a mussy on us, this canna be I.'"

"I know just what you mean." Veronica smiled. "Wouldn't he just be surprised if he saw us sitting here!"

"Geoffrey? He certainly would. D'you think we ought to be grateful to him, Veronica?"

Now she laughed. "No way! Hardly his doing we met . . . I've not said sorry properly for being such a clot, Patience."

"No need."

"That foul paint. Or haven't you found it? I do hope you

162

haven't." But Patience's face answered her. "Christ, I'm sorry! You didn't fall or anything? Hurt yourself?"

"No, honestly, it was all right, you mustn't mind. I had someone with me; we were going down for a bottle of wine. I won't pretend it didn't give us a turn, but it was all right, being two of us."

"Well, thank God for that. I'll clean it up in the morning. Am I really going to stay with you, Patience?"

"As long as you want to. Not a day longer." She had been thinking about this.

"Cool," said Veronica.

After her look at the sea, which she pronounced tame after St Ives, Veronica talked Patience into a dark charcoal skirt and very expensive pair of trousers, both from Jaeger, and they then decided they had enough to carry and headed for home. "Let's walk the last bit," said Veronica as they came out of Leyning station. "It's not worth a taxi from here."

"No, I always walk," said Patience; but it was strange to walk up through the graveyard together.

"Only twenty-four hours," said Veronica. "And now look at us."

"Hard to believe, isn't it?"

"But good. I wonder what we'll fight over first. Bound to be something."

"Oh, I do hope not. I hate fights."

"Sometimes one must," said Veronica.

They had turned into the High Street and were almost home when Mrs Vansittart came hurrying across the road to waylay them. "You have been busy, my dear." She looked at their parcels as she spoke to Patience. "And this is your young friend?"

"Yes, this is Veronica Lavolle. She's going to stay with me for a while." Patience moved forward, hoping to end the conversation there, but Mrs Vansittart fell in beside them.

"One of the Cornish Lavolles, my dear?" she asked Veronica. "It's not a common name, is it? I have an old friend lives in Penzance; she writes so admiringly of the dear old Duke. Says he's an absolute pillar of society, the church, the lot. And quite an age, too. He must be well over eighty and still doing his bit. So sad there's no son to inherit, take some of the load off his shoulders. You'll be a cousin, I suppose?" Getting no response, she turned back to Patience, who had got out her front door key. "You had another caller this afternoon, by the way. I was waiting for the electrician and noticed her. Tall and thin, dark hair and dark glasses. I expect you'll find she left a note. She certainly came back a couple of times. But I mustn't keep you, loaded down like that. You certainly have been shopping, haven't you?"

"Poor Veronica lost her luggage." Patience put her key in the lock, the description of her caller niggling at her mind.

"British Rail, I suppose, or whatever they call themselves these days. Hopeless, inefficient lot. But I mustn't keep you standing there. Do come in and have a drink with me tonight, both of you. I'll expect you about six; how nice."

"A royal command," said Veronica, safe indoors.

"I'm afraid so. I don't quite know why, but she is one of Leyning's great ladies. What she says, goes."

"And you can hardly tell her we've a date, when she'll be looking out the window to see what we do. But she was wrong about the note, so she doesn't actually know everything."

"Note?"

"Your dark-haired caller. Did you recognise the description?"

"No." Again that niggle at the back of her mind. "But, Veronica, are you really kin of a duke?"

"Worse than that. I'm his granddaughter. Strictly illegit, of course. And it was his always being such a pillar of the state made me so hard for them to bear, see."

"Yes, I do see. And I'm afraid I understand the way Geoffrey behaved a whole lot better."

"I thought you would." They were silent for a moment, both contemplating the unattractive truth. "He wanted the Duke's daughter, with no illegitimate strings attached, and Mum wasn't having that. No way. Bless her. And it's all so absurd. Dukes are as dead as dodos. Deader. Dodos still have some shelf life in museums, but who wants a stuffed duke?"

"Who indeed? But, Veronica, what on earth are we going to tell Mrs Vansittart tonight?"

"Why not the truth?" said Veronica.

"Oh! I never thought of that."

"It would save a hell of a lot of trouble. I mean, not about the bag of flour, please! I couldn't bear anyone to know about that."

"No, no, of course not. No one ever shall. And that's a promise. Well." She thought about it. "You know, you might have something there. It would make things so much simpler. I'd been thinking of all kinds of stories about your being a young cousin of Geoffrey's I'd never heard of, that sort of thing. But to have to keep it up for the rest of our lives . . ."

"You're really thinking long-term aren't you? It's cool. But you're the one has to decide, Patience. I'm used to it, see. I've been a bastard all my life. I can wear it. It's you it'll come hard on, raised eyebrows all round, all that, but don't you think it might be easier in the end?"

"You're absolutely right. I'll feel God's own fool for a bit, with everyone so sorry for me, but it won't last for ever. Besides," – she had had time to work this out – "I'm not sure there's really much alternative. Once Mrs Vansittart writes to her cousin in Penzance she's sure to put two and two together and come up with the whole story. We might just as well make a virtue of necessity. One thing – if we tell her tonight, the whole town will know tomorrow and that will save trouble."

"Cool." Veronica looked at her watch. "If we're due at six we ought to start changing, oughtn't we? I bet the old dear expects her guests dressed up and dead on time. She won't be writing to her cousin in Penzance anyway, phoning more likely, but she'll wait till after six so we ought to get in first, bit of luck. Are you going to wear the trousers or the skirt?"

"Oh, the skirt," said Patience, amusedly aware of being bullied for her own good. Obeying instructions, she liked the result, and Veronica, joining her in new jeans and shirt, smiled her approval. "But your lipstick's the wrong colour, and you need some eyebrows. Hang on a mo." She went deftly to work. "There" – standing back to admire the results – "see?"

"Yes, I do see. You've got an eye all right, Veronica. I never thought I could wear red."

"We'll get you a suit a bit later, but I think we'd need to go to London for that. There was a place Mum used to go to off Bond Street."

Was there indeed? But Patience kept the thought to herself. She was beginning to get an oddish picture of Veronica's mother, the Duke's daughter. "It's time we went," she said instead.

She had wondered which of her big front rooms Mrs Vansittart would choose to entertain them in and was not surprised to be ushered into the more elegant of the two, the one with glass-fronted cabinets full of probably priceless china rather than books.

Responding to Mrs Vansittart's greeting, she suddenly realised just how awkward this occasion was going to be, and caught a rueful glance from Veronica suggesting that the same thing had struck her. The curtains were drawn against the early autumn darkness, but they were sitting with their drinks in the bay window that commanded such a good daytime view of the street, and Mrs Vansittart's question about her afternoon caller came naturally enough.

"No," Patience answered it, "she didn't come back, and there wasn't a note. I can't think who it can have been. Not many people know my new address yet. I've got terribly behind with things because the Hall sold so fast and I had to move. I got the change of address cards from the man you recommended, Mrs Vansittart, but I'm ashamed to say I've hardly sent any of them yet."

"I could do that for you." Veronica put her orange juice down carefully on the little mat that protected the marquetry table. "One thing the sisters did teach us at my school was to write what they called a good clear hand."

"Convent school, of course. And a very good education, too." Mrs Vansittart approved. "So you're a Catholic, my dear, like the rest of your family."

"Not any more, I'm not." Veronica put down her glass and stood up. "May I use your loo, please?"

"Of course." Mrs Vansittart concealed surprise like a lady. "Down the hall and right by the garden door."

"Thanks." She gave Patience a speaking look, and left the room.

Patience took the plunge. "Sensible child," she said. "She's giving me a chance to explain to you, Mrs Vansittart. It's been a shock to me. It will be a shock to you, too, I'm afraid. My first thought was to say nothing, try to cover up, but we've talked about it and decided it's bound to come out sooner or later, so better sooner." She took a steadying breath. "You asked about Veronica and the Lavolles, and you are quite right, she's the Duke's granddaughter, but illegitimate."

"Oh!" said Mrs Vansittart. And then: "That youngest daughter! Jessica? – No, Jennifer. I remember my cousin saying something. And she never would name the father."

"No," said Patience bleakly. "He was my husband."

"Oh, my dear—" For the first time, Mrs Vansittart used the words as if she meant them. "I am so very sorry. You didn't know?"

"No. If I had I would have divorced him. Veronica is eighteen years old, Mrs Vansittart, but it had been going on much longer. Ever since Suez. Since her mother was younger than Veronica is now." Oddly, in the catharsis of speech, she felt bound to defend Veronica's mother.

"What a terrible thing. Just think of all those speeches he used to make, about family values! Do you remember? – Of course you do. I beg your pardon, my dear. It hits you hardest of all and I can see you are taking it quite beautifully. How long have you known?"

"Since Veronica came to me yesterday. I hope she is going to let me adopt her. Her mother is dead, you see—"

"And the family?"

"Veronica won't go to them because of the way they treated her mother."

"Oh, my goodness . . . But here she comes!" She turned to greet Veronica. "My dear, I am so very sorry about your mother. You must let us all do everything we can to help you be happy with Mrs Crankshaw."

"Oh, I shall, thank you. I mean to be."

"Did you see how beautifully she changed the subject?" asked Veronica, back at home over an omelette. "You were dead right: she's a great lady. With not enough to do, poor thing."

"I know. It's true of all of us. Someone needs to harness the energies of the old. To treadmills if nothing else offers. We're so wasted!"

"You're not old, Patience, and don't try to behave as if you were. It was a pleasure to see old Ma Vansittart taking in your new outfit. How soon can we go to London and buy you that suit?"

"Not till we have got a few things sorted out here. Your A levels, for a start; we must lose no time about that. And I must see Mr Jones and get him working on what happened about your mother's money. I can't believe even Geoffrey would have left you totally unprovided for."

"Mr Jones?"

"My solicitor; such a nice man. He lives down the High Street."

"Here in Leyning? Don't you have someone looking after all that money?"

"Geoffrey did. Mr Jones is finding someone."

"Ouch." She pulled a face which turned into a yawn. "You

look tired, Patience, and I'm knackered. All that bracing Brighton ozone, d'you think? Shall we be slobs and stack the dishes and go to bed?"

"Yes, it's been a long day. I admit I am a bit tired. We'll both be better for a long night."

But in the morning she woke with a small niggling headache and lay for a few moments wondering if she could be starting flu.

No time for that. She got herself firmly out of bed and discovered she had forgotten to open her bedroom window, which doubtless explained the headache. She thought Veronica looked heavy-eyed, too, when she joined her for breakfast. "Let's have a quiet day today," she said, pouring coffee.

"Let things settle a bit," agreed Veronica. "Cool. No, I won't have an egg today, thanks, just a bit of toast. That's all I usually have."

"Funny to know so little about each other," said Patience.

"I reckon we know the things that count. But, yes, there's going to be some ground to cover. Like do you watch the Teletubbies or the Simpsons?"

"Neither," said Patience. "But I like to get the six o'clock news."

"Mum watched a lot of soaps. I'm not into it much. Boring." She stifled a yawn. "I'm falling asleep again. May we get the dishes done, Patience, so I can get going in the cellar? I'll feel better when I've done that."

"It's going to be a horrid job, I'm afraid." Patience turned on the hot tap.

"And serve me bloody well right. Sorry! Why don't you have a dishwasher, Patience?"

"No room. Anyway, I quite like doing dishes. Specially at this sink, with its view of the garden. We must get some more nuts for the birds when we go out."

"I like the way you say 'we'," said Veronica. "When are we going to go out?"

"When you're done in the cellar? There are all kinds of things I need for the house. It was all so different at the Hall. Goodness, it's hard to believe it's only five days since I left there."

"Don't tell me you're homesick?"

"Good gracious, no way! If I never see that place again, it will be too soon. Lord, it's good to have you here to say that to, Veronica. Promise you won't let me batten on you?"

"Batten? Not just your line surely."

"Well, don't let me bully you either. I mean, maybe you don't want to come out shopping."

"'Course I do. The least I can do is carry for you, when you're feeding me."

"I like feeding you." In her turn, she swallowed a yawn. "Are you sure you want to do the cellar today? It's going to be a pig of a job."

"It'll get worse with leaving. Have you any old rags I can use for the turps?"

"Oh dear, not a thing. It never occurred to me to bring those."

"Well you didn't know you were getting a poltergeist with the house, did you?"

"That's just what it felt like!" Patience smiled at her. "I know! Why don't you use that drippy skirt for rags? I really don't think I want to see you in it again."

"I should rather think not."

"Unless you think you ought to send it back to the friend who lent it to you?"

"No." It came out explosively. "I shan't be seeing that lot again. That's the other reason I came away. What I didn't know, when I went to them, was they're on the hard stuff. They took my purse; that's why I had to hitch up here."

"You hitched! Oh, Veronica. Promise you won't ever again. It's too dangerous."

"Not looking the way I did, it wasn't. Well, one of them was a bit off, but you've got to be able to cope. And the last one gave me a fiver. *Not* for services rendered, in case you were wondering. He came from Newlyn, said he wouldn't want a nice St Ives girl loose in Brighton with no money. Truckers are OK mostly; it's private cars are dodgy. OK—" grinning at Patience as she dried the last teaspoon – "never again and that's a promise. Where did you put the turps?"

"Still in its bag in the front hall, I think." Patience unbolted the cellar door as Veronica tore strips from the sad skirt. "Promise to leave it if it's impossible, Veronica; we can always get a man in, after all."

"Anything he can do I can do better," said Veronica cheerfully, rolling up her sleeves. "No, I can manage, thanks." She picked up turps, scraper and rags. "Why don't you sit down for a bit? You look a bit off this morning, tell you the truth."

"I've felt better," admitted Patience. "I do hope I'm not starting something." She finished polishing the table and was glad to sit down beside it with the newspaper, while Veronica vanished down the cellar stair.

"It stinks of paint down here," came her cheerful voice. "No wonder you weren't fooled." And then: "That's funny . . ."

She reappeared a minute later to find Patience nodding

over the newspaper. "Wake up," she said. "There's something blocking the vent down there; that's why we're so sleepy. It's the boiler." She found the front door key on the hall shelf and swung the door wide. "Yes," – looking down into the sunk area beside the steps – "something's fallen on to the vent. It wasn't like that the other day or I could never have got the paint down. Come and look, Patience, fresh air's what you need."

Patience had been on the verge of drifting off to sleep, but pulled herself reluctantly out of her chair and moved slowly out to join Veronica at the top of the front steps.

"Don't fall in!" Veronica put a steadying arm round her waist. "You need a grating over it, Patience. It looks like somebody's rubbish down there. What sluts people are. Missed the dustmen, I suppose, and just dropped it in. And it's cut off the air supply to the boiler, see? You read about it in the papers: whole families dying in caravans with faulty heating."

"What an extraordinary thing." Patience was breathing great gulps of fresh air and feeling better by the minute. "Do be careful." She hung on to the door jamb as Veronica let go of her and climbed down into the area.

"It's just a bag full of newspapers." She picked up the black bag and heaved it up on to the pavement. "How very odd."

"I don't like it a bit," said Patience. "Bring it indoors, Veronica – quick, before anyone notices." She glanced swiftly across the road.

"She went out shopping," said Veronica.

Back in the house, Patience went straight to the back door and threw it wide open. "Would you be a dear and open all the windows upstairs? But don't sit down or anything!"

"I sure won't. Should we leave the front door for a bit, do you think? Get a through draught?"

"Don't you think the windows should do it, if we stay out for a while?"

"Get the shopping done now, while it clears? Now you've got that bolt on the back gate we could perfectly well leave the back door open while we are out."

"I suppose we could." Patience propped a chair against the back door to hold it open against the draught that rushed through the house when Veronica opened the front windows upstairs.

"I managed to get the attic window open," said Veronica, returning. "You ought to do something with all that space, Patience. How do you feel?"

"Better."

"So do I. But should we call the Gas Board, do you think?"

"I don't really see why. They'd take forever to come, and we'd have to stay in for them, and we do know exactly what happened. They made me put in that grille, you know, after I had the boiler installed. When they tested it, it didn't draw properly, and it was the grille or no boiler. You're absolutely right, I should have had a grating put across the top, but I was afraid it might mean planning permission and all that hassle; you've no idea how fierce they are in this High Street."

"I can imagine," said Veronica. "You can hardly change a door knob in St Ives without a fuss. When are your dustbins emptied, Patience?"

"That's the funny thing," said Patience. "Tomorrow."

Ten

"**B**ut you really ought to tell someone," said Veronica, not for the first time, over their lunch of salad and cheese. "Like, I keep thinking, if you hadn't had the heating switched to go off at night, we might not have waked up this morning."

"I don't think it works like that." Patience had been thinking about this. "The boiler was on all night, after all, it's just the radiators go off. It's a slow build-up, isn't it? You had your window open, didn't you? I forgot mine. But it was your going down to the cellar saved us. Lucky for me you came."

"Lucky for me too. Look, I know it seems crazy, and it has to have been an accident, but don't you think maybe you ought to tell the police?"

"You say that?" Patience temporised. "I thought you young hated the police?"

"Like pigs, you mean? Fuzz? All that? I've always found them OK."

"Well, I suppose in St Ives they knew who you were."

"For what it was worth? I suppose they did. So: good old English snobbery at work, you mean?"

"Just that. Geoffrey was a policeman when we met."

"I never knew that. I thought he was just a leisured gent."

175

"That was after he married me," said Patience. "Before, he was working his way up at Scotland Yard. But it didn't happen fast enough for him. Nothing ever did, poor Geoffrey . . . I've never liked the police much. You see, I was accused of murder once. Clapped in the cells, in Lewes, under the Magistrate's Court."

"You have to be joking!"

"No. It's true. I was twenty-one – not much older than you are. There was capital punishment then. I sat in that cell, facing the gallows. I was sick with fright, Veronica. Not fair to blame the police; it seemed such a clear case. Of course they treated me like a guilty thing, worthless, who'd killed an old lady for her money."

"Money?"

"Yes. I was her companion. It's a long story. She made a will, you see, to tease her relations, leaving it all to me. I was a relation too, actually. And then she died – poisoned – and everything pointed to me. It was hard not to believe it myself, sitting in that cell. Then Geoffrey read about it at the Yard – we knew each other a bit – and he came down like St George and the Dragon. He had one bit of evidence that helped my case, and then I got thinking and we talked about it, and he looked at it with a fresh eye, believing me. He would have been a good policeman, Veronica; it was all such a pity. Money spoils people."

"So what happened?"

"He went through the evidence against me with a fine-tooth comb, and it didn't stand up. How could it? So they let me out. Goodness, that was a strange day: the doors opening, the change in my gaolers, the grovelling. I think they were afraid I'd sue for wrongful arrest, but there wasn't so much of that about in those days. Besides, I hadn't actually been arrested, they kept saying that, just 'held for questioning'. It felt like arrest to me. I've not been mad keen on policemen since. Though of course all that lot retired years ago."

"Brave of you to come back to the Hall."

"I didn't want to. But Geoffrey wanted to live there. It suited the image he'd planned. He talked me into it. I'd have been better without all that money too. I should have gone back to college – I was in my last year when it all happened. But it was all so awful: the whole family lined up against me, conspiring, it felt like. Well, I was the outsider; you couldn't blame them for closing ranks against me." Her mind shied away from the picture of that hostile group, and Mark among them, his eyes avoiding hers.

"So who had done it? What happened?"

"Geoffrey discovered that the old lady was coming down with senile dementia, or thought she was. And she had forged a lot of the evidence against me herself, so as to get a hold on me. She was such an old tartar, the other companions had always left, but I stood up to her. I think she liked it actually; up to a point. But she had to have everyone under her thumb. When I refused to report on her family to her she forged her own signature on a cheque and landed me with it. I gave in for the moment – anything to get through Christmas – but I was going to leave right after. Only then she died. There had been a forged prescription, too, for the sleeping pills that killed her. You can see how black it looked for me, until Geoffrey turned up and went to work on it."

"So what happened?"

"In the end the coroner ruled that it was suicide while the balance of her mind was disturbed, or some woolly

177

phrase like that. So then of course I inherited all her money."

"That can't have pleased her family."

"No, poor things. It was hideous for them. They had counted on it so. And that hadn't been good for them either. She'd kept them all dangling on her strings. A horrid business. Money really is the root of all evil."

"Lack of it's no fun either. But it's not just the money bothers you, is it? Like, there's something else."

"It was the way they ganged up on me. The whole lot of them. I didn't ever want to see them again."

"And have you?"

"Not till just the other day. The day we met, actually. My cousin Mary suddenly showed up on the doorstep. It was her turning against me I'd minded most, her and her brother. She was on her way to the ferry to meet him in France somewhere. Said it was time we buried the hatchet. And we did. It was good. She stayed to lunch, and we talked about it a bit. She told me she and Mark had been going to break ranks, as she called it, meant to stand up for me if it had come to a trial. I don't know how much good it would have done me, and of course one will never know—"

"Whether they really would have? No way. Easy to say it after the event. You liked them?"

"They were the best of the lot. Mary had got away, had a flat of her own in town, and a job, and a string of young men. In those days, of course, she got engaged to them, one after the other. She brought one down that Christmas and married him after it was all over, but it didn't work out. It was their mother asked me to go there in the first place. I never could like her. She was tough as old army boots, Josephine Brigance."

"And the brother – what was he like?"

"Mark?" Was she blushing? Could she after all these years? "He had all the charm in the world, and used it. I'm not sure charm isn't almost as dangerous as money; you get to think you can get away with murder." And then, horrified: "No, that's not what I meant at all."

"'Course not. What did he do, this charming Mark?"

"Damn all, so far as I could see. He'd done awfully well at Cambridge, his mother kept saying, and had just been idling about at home since he came down." He had offered to get a job for her sake. Top hat or bowler, he had asked lightly, surely not meaning it. She did not want to talk about Mark. "If you could call Featherstone Hall home." She changed the subject. "It did not feel much like it to me. Horrible house."

"And yet you lived there all those years, afterwards."

"Yes; it's hard to believe, now, knowing about you and your mother."

"But you didn't. And I suppose he had charm too, my father, when you come right down to it."

"Oh dear me, yes. But a totally different kind from Mark's. Geoffrey was the 'I'm just a helpless little boy, you must look after me' kind. Mark was your Byronic man, the world his oyster. You could imagine him swash-buckling his way through a romantic novel. Women swooning all over him. That kind of thing." She felt she was achieving just the light touch she needed.

"Did you swoon?"

"Well, a bit. That's why I minded it so much when I found he and Mary were part of the cabal against me."

"Like, you fell into Father's arms on the rebound? That

figures. And he gave you no time to change your mind. He was always a quick operator, was Father."

"He said he wanted to take me away from it all."

"'Course he did. You and the money. What happened to romantic Mark then?"

"Do you know, the most surprising thing. Mary was telling me the other day. She was off to meet him in France because he went into something very cloak and dagger indeed. The only way to see him is by assignation somewhere in Europe. And he must be good at it too. Well, he would be. They won't let him retire."

"Charming the secret birds off the trees. Cool. I'd like to meet your Mark."

"Hardly my Mark."

"But nobody else's?"

"Well, no marriage, Mary said. But what that means these days—"

"Damn all," said Veronica cheerfully.

It gave Patience the courage to ask a question that had been simmering in her mind. "How about you, Veronica? Have you a . . ." She hesitated, looking for the right word.

"Like, boyfriend? Partner? Man? Mate?" suggested Veronica. "Thought I had, till I went to him in trouble and he pinched my purse. Aren't I glad I was too busy looking after Mum to fall into bed with him like he wanted."

"I'm glad too," said Patience. "So we don't have to worry about that."

"No way. Actually, Patience, it taught me something. Like, it's awfully uncool, but I don't reckon I'm going to sleep with anyone till I know them a hell of a lot better than that."

"You mean, you haven't?"

"Isn't it quaint? Tell me, just when did you say your cousin Mary turned up out of the blue?"

"Two days ago. The day you and I met."

"That's what I thought you said. So it was after I dumped that paint in the cellar?"

"Yes. In fact she and I found it together, when we went down for a bottle of wine. Actually, she said something about having seen a teenager hanging around. I suppose that was you."

"So she knew about the grille. It might have given her the idea."

"Mary? But she was on her way to the ferry."

"She said. She could perfectly well have hung around, collected the bag of papers, come back later on, dumped it down when we were at Mrs Vansittart's or even the day before. We were both dead to the world, remember; we'd never have noticed."

"But we didn't feel anything yesterday."

"We've no idea how long it takes to build up. You said so yourself."

"But it's absurd. Why Mary? And after all these years, too."

"Because something's changed," said Veronica.

"Well, I suppose everything's changed; that's true enough. Look at us."

"Ah," said Veronica, "but Mary didn't know you and I were going to get together, on account of it hadn't happened. So that wasn't it. Father's death, yes, that might have had something to do with it. Or your moving here? Maybe no one could get at you when you were at the Hall with all those smarmy servants."

181

"But why, Veronica?"

"You've always wondered if my father was right about the old lady's death, haven't you? It came over loud and clear when you told me about it. You were so careful what you said. You didn't say she committed suicide. You said that was what the coroner decided. And that was why you didn't want to see any of them. You didn't trust them, and you seem to have been dead right. Tell me, do you think Father wondered too?"

"Veronica, I just don't know. We never talked about it. I think that was one of the things that went wrong between us."

"I should just about think it might be. So who *did* you think had done it?"

"All of them together. It seemed the only way it could have happened. Making me the scapegoat, see? If I'd been found guilty of the old lady's murder, I couldn't have inherited her estate – and it would have been divided among them as next of kin. Sitting in that cell, I even started wondering if they could have got me down on purpose. She kept changing her will, you understand. It was all left to the fifty-two letter alphabet when I got there. And that would have done no one any good."

"And did it work out?"

"Yes. She changed her will almost at once. In my favour. So that she could hold it over me."

"Not a nice old lady."

"She wasn't. But bullying her family was the way she managed to enjoy her life, and you have to respect her for that. Not bad still to be an active functioning tyrant in your nineties."

"You don't in the least believe she killed herself, do you?"

"No. I'm afraid I don't. But it's years ago, Veronica. Mary

told me that the older generation of Ffeatherses are mostly dead or in homes."

"And the younger ones?"

"Well, Mary and Mark you know about."

"If you believe Mary. And who else?"

"Ludwig and Leonora. They were Seward Ffeathers' children – he was the older son. Their father wanted them to be musicians, hence the names, but they were mad on science. They've totally vanished into the United States, Mary said. Not so much as a Christmas card."

"Sinister?"

"Not necessarily. Their father's senile; they may have seen it coming and wanted out from under. It would be like them."

"What about their mother?"

"She was always a complete nonentity, but Mary says she took on a new lease of life when Seward went downhill: had him sectioned and is doing her own thing at last. I don't know what form it takes."

"So she's not in a home. A question mark over her. And over the vanished children. After all, if they were into science they might have been able to whip up the slow-acting miracle poison no one could trace."

"It was just an overdose of her own pills. The problem was, how had she got it, if I hadn't given it to her. Which I didn't."

"I believe you," said Veronica. "Who else is there?"

"Just Priss. Now that was a surprise. She was Joseph Ffeathers' daughter – he was the younger son. She wanted to train as a social worker, that was the kind of person she was, but old Mrs Ffeathers wouldn't put up the money. So she just hung around at the Hall and her mother kept dragging young men down for her, and no good came of it. And all the time she was carrying on with another cousin, Mrs Ffeathers' lawyer. Mary told me about it the other day. Secret assignations and lurking in corridors, all that. They got married after the old lady died, and everyone was flabbergasted, Mary said. Well, so was I; she was such a white mouse of a girl and he was very much the man of the world. Older, of course, running his own firm. He was my cousin too, and my trustee. Geoffrey and I always thought it was his fault somehow that all my money vanished while I was growing up, but Geoffrey said there was no way we could prove it. He said I'd had trouble enough already without a long legal battle getting nowhere but lawyers' fees. And after all, I had old Mrs Ffeathers' money by then so it really didn't matter."

"I keep wondering what you did about the money."

"What I did?"

"Like, they all seem to have managed all right without it. Going off to America, marrying shady young lawyers, settling comfortably into old people's homes. You gave them some of it, didn't you?"

"Well, of course I did. How could I not? Mrs Ffeathers hadn't in the least meant me to have it. It was just part of the game she played. I found a new lawyer, Mr Jones here in Leyning, who saw my point of view, and we settled annuities on the lot of them. Wonderful to have so much that I could. Geoffrey was furious."

"I bet he was. Not what he meant at all. I say, you haven't left any of the rest of it back to them in your will, have you, since he died? Have you let them know it? Or might they think you had?"

"I can't think how. I told you, till the other day I'd seen none of them since it all happened."

"You haven't answered my question, Patience."

"Are you bullying me?"

"Trying to. Strictly for your own good. You have, haven't you? It stands to reason you would. And somebody's guessed it, or found out, and got impatient. And Mary's the one who was here."

"I don't believe it."

"You mean, you won't believe it."

"I suppose I do." They had finished their lunch by now. "Let's have some coffee." She got up to put on the kettle. "If Mary caught the ferry, she's out of it. The snag is – I feel the most complete fool – I didn't get her address. She said she'd be in touch and we left it at that. I was a bit off balance that day."

"My fault," said Veronica. "I'm sorry. The police could find out, Patience."

"I am not going to the police."

"I told you we'd quarrel sooner or later," said Veronica cheerfully. "It seems to be sooner. But you're the boss. Mind you, one thing we could do is look up Ffeathers in the London phone book. I shouldn't think there'd be many of them. Or Brigances, come to that. Ring them and see where they were the other night. Have you got one?"

"London phone book? Yes, an old one. It's on the shelf in my bedroom."

"I'll get it."

As she ran upstairs the front door bell rang and Patience turned off the kettle and went to answer it.

"Mary!" she exclaimed. And then, looking past her: "My

goodness – Mark!" Just for a moment she had not been sure. The black hair was shockingly white above black eyebrows, the good bones stronger than ever in the tanned face.

"He would come," said Mary. "When I told him about your haunt, he said I shouldn't have left you on your own like that. We've been burning up the road to get here. It's good to find you're OK, Patience."

"Well, up to a point." Patience stepped back to usher them in. "I can't tell you how glad I am to see you both. It's been a long time, Mark." She held out her hand. "You don't look old enough."

"I feel it." His warm hand clasped hers. "And let's hope we have both changed for the better. A brave cousin would kiss you, Patience."

"Would he?" Patience shut the door behind him. "Here's my haunt." Veronica was coming down the stairs with the telephone book. "May I introduce Veronica Lavolle, Geoffrey's illegitimate daughter. Veronica, we don't need that. Here are Mary and Mark Brigance, come to make sure I'm all right. We were just going to look you up in the London book, Mary," she explained. "Something rather sinister happened here after you left, and Veronica suspected you. Come in." She ushered them into the dining room. "I was just going to make some coffee. Get some more cups, Veronica, would you? And the biscuit tin . . . You've had lunch?"

"Yes, on the ferry." Mary shed her jacket and settled at the dining table. "And very nasty it was. Nice to meet you, Veronica, but aren't you rather a surprise? And what exactly did you suspect me of?"

"She's turned out to be a wonderfully nice surprise,"

Patience said. "Once we'd explained ourselves. Her mother died, you see, and she thought it was all my fault."

"Whereas it was Geoffrey Crankshaw's, of course," said Mark. "I never could like that man, Patience, though I suppose that's not altogether surprising. How old are you, Veronica?"

"Everyone asks that." Veronica passed him the biscuit tin. "And the answer is eighteen, but it had been going on for years before that."

"Oh, Patience," said Mary.

"I'm getting used to it." It was almost true. "And look at the bonus I've got out of it. Veronica is going to come and live with me," she told them. "We're going to fix up for her to do the A levels she missed because her mother was ill."

"And we've just had our first difference," said Veronica. "If you don't ask them, Patience, I shall." She handed Mary a cup of coffee. "You caught the ferry that day you lunched here?" she asked.

"Of course I did. I met Mark according to plan, and here we are as a result. But why do you ask?"

"Because of the sinister thing that happened," said Mark. "What was it, Patience?"

"Somebody dropped a bag of newspapers on to the air vent from the cellar," Patience told him. "The one Veronica poured the paint through. We both felt a bit strange this morning and luckily Veronica went down to clear up the paint and saw what had happened. I'm afraid she thought—"

"It had given me a bright idea," said Mary. "But why, Patience?"

"Ancient history," said Mark. "That's what I was afraid of.

187

But it wasn't us two, Veronica, and we could prove it easily enough."

"Natch," said Veronica. "I feel a proper clot."

"You shouldn't. You were thinking on exactly the right lines. I've been afraid, always, that something would churn it all up again. It was too good to be true, that coroner's finding, wasn't it, Patience?"

"You knew?"

"I'm more ashamed of that than of anything I ever did. Yes, I knew. It was my mother, you see. I heard her say something to Uncle Joseph, that first dreadful morning. I was numb with shock that day, taking it in. They had to be in it, all three of them, she and Joseph and Seward. Got you down; hoped Gran would leave it all to you; and then . . . Their own mother."

"Sick," said Veronica.

"But how did they do it?" asked Patience.

"I hardly dared even wonder, for fear Geoffrey Crankshaw would read my mind, but I always thought it must have been something cooked up by Ludwig and Leonora – a slow-acting capsule, or something. They vanished pretty quickly to the States afterwards and were never heard from again. Those days when you were in gaol were the worst of my life, Patience."

"I didn't enjoy them very much myself."

"And then Crankshaw turned up, thank God, and proved it suicide, and I didn't need to speak up after all, and send my mother to prison. I told Mary I was sure you were innocent; we just needed to wait a bit, I hoped."

"I couldn't understand why," Mary joined in. "You should have told me, Mark; I wouldn't have let you wait."

"I know. That's why I didn't. I'm sorry, Patience, sorrier

than I can say. I've wanted to tell you that ever since, but you wouldn't see us, afterwards, and I couldn't blame you. It's been on my mind always; unfinished business, a running sore—"

"But why should it break out again now?" asked Mary.

"That's what Veronica and I were wondering." Patience poured more coffee for them all. "We think it has to do with Geoffrey's death."

"It's hard to see why." Mark reached out for a biscuit. "The case could hardly be more closed. I'm sure Mother and Uncle Joseph were the moving spirits in the plot against you, Patience, and they're both dead. Seward and Emily are out of it; what brains they had are gone for good. Which leaves Grisel of the older generation, and she has been a surprise. But they'd never have let her in on the plot, not the droop she was then."

"What about Priss?" Patience began, but Veronica interrupted her.

"You've got to tell them, Patience. Or if you won't, I will. I don't think it's ancient history at all." She turned to Mark. "Isn't there a statute of something-or-other about old crimes? You can't drag them up again? And this one really is old as the hills. No, I think it's Patience's lunatic will has started things up again."

"Will?" Mark asked.

"If I worked it out, surely you can. Who do you think she has left all that money back to, now Father is dead?"

"Oh, Veronica . . ." Patience felt herself slowly turning scarlet.

But Mark was laughing. "Bright girl, Veronica. You're quite right, we should have worked it out. And you think one of us has done so, and is getting impatient? It might be true, at that," he went on, "but thank God it's not Mary or me. Well, that settles it, Mar; we'll confirm those bookings at the Black Stag, and you two must dine there with us tonight. Meanwhile I'll get on the phone and act the returning prodigal ringing round the family to get back in touch and find out in passing where they all were – when, Patience?"

"Last night or the night before, we think it must have been. And that reminds me of something. What about Mrs Vansittart's dark lady, Veronica? The one who didn't leave a note. She never did come back."

"Unless it was to drop the bag down," said Veronica. "And scarper."

"Who's Mrs Vansittart?" asked Mark. "And what dark lady?"

"Mrs Vansittart's a neighbour across the road," Patience told him. "Veronica and I went shopping in Brighton yesterday and when we got back she told us she had seen this dark-haired, dark-glassed woman ringing at my doorbell and generally hanging around."

"A bit late in the season for dark glasses," said Mary.

"That's what I thought."

"What sort of age?"

"Well, Mrs Vansittart obviously thought it was a friend of mine, so our age, kind of."

"So it could be Leonora or Priss," said Mark. "I'll tell you one thing, Patience; I'm going to tell all the family that you are changing your will, and you must do it."

"Oh, I'm going to," said Patience. "I'm seeing my solicitor tomorrow."

"Good." He looked at his watch. "Come on, Mar, time to go

and face the smell of gravy at the Black Stag. I didn't believe it could still hang around there after all these years, but it does. What time would you like to eat, Patience?"

"Seven thirty maybe? But come here for a drink first. Any time after six."

"Splendid. And if the postman brings you a parcel of poisoned chocolates between now and then, don't eat them, either of you. Good to meet you, Veronica; I hope you are going to be a niece to Mary and me."

"Cool," said Veronica, showing them out. And then, rejoining Patience: "Wow!"

"Isn't he?" agreed Patience.

"It's something about the brown skin and the white hair and the instant decisions, I reckon. If he wants to drag me off to his cave, I'll go. I liked Mary, too, but of course we've only got their word for it that they were on the ferry like they said."

"Oh, Veronica!"

"It's true, but I'm like you, I don't believe it for a minute. So where does that leave us?"

"Baffled."

"Not altogether, you know. Think, Patience! At least you know your instinct was right. The old lady's death was murder, by a group of them, just like you thought. And you can't honestly blame Mark for not wanting to split on his mum, can you?"

"No, of course not." After trying for so long to forget that hostile group she had found united against her on the morning of Mrs Ffeathers' death, now she was trying to remember the individual faces and their expressions. No use. She could not. She had been too shocked to notice more than Mark's withdrawal.

191

"It's all such a long time ago," said Veronica, reading her mind. "Best forgotten, don't you think? Water under the dam? All that. Or do I mean the bridge? Whatever, the thing is it's now we need to think about, not old then. I'm sure Mark'll find your dark lady for you and sort her out, now he's into it. I bet he's sorted worse things than that in his time, wouldn't you think?"

"Yes." She spoke mechanically. Her mind was spinning out of control. She could not talk about Mark. She picked up her coffee cup and stacked it with Veronica's.

"No." Veronica reached out gently to take it from her. "You look knackered, Patience, and I don't wonder. I'm going to make you a hot water bottle and tuck you up in bed." She moved across the room to put on the kettle.

"Oh, goodness, what a lovely idea!" Patience felt a sheen of tears behind her eyes. "The bottle's in the top drawer." And, taking it: "What a kind child you are, Veronica."

"I intend to be."

It was good to be alone. She lay flat on her back for a while, thinking about nothing so far as she could manage it, then got up and went over to the little writing desk in the corner of the room and sat down to work out the details of her new will. Geoffrey had told her once that an entirely handwritten will – holograph, he had called it – would be legally valid. She made it short and clear. Her entire estate halved between Veronica, and Mark and Mary, who were to act as trustees for Veronica until she was twenty-five. Then she picked up the telephone by her bed and dialled Mrs Vansittart's number.

"I'm just nipping across the road to get Mrs Vansittart to witness my new will," she told Veronica, emerging from her bedroom. "Her housekeeper's there, so there are two of them."

"Ask her if she's seen the dark lady again," said Veronica.

"Good idea. I will."

"And don't let her keep you too long, gossiping. I'm sure the Black Stag expects its dinner guests in their handsome best."

"You're bullying me again. I begin to think perhaps I like it."

"While it lasts," said Veronica, and Patience crossed the road wondering what she meant.

Mrs Vansittart rather thought she had seen the dark-haired woman somewhere in town, but was surprised that she had left no note and never returned to Patience's house.

"It's odd, isn't it? Thank you." Patience picked up her duly witnessed document, smiling back at the cheerful housekeeper. "She must have changed her mind, for some reason, I suppose. And now I must run, Mrs Vansittart; I've cousins staying at the Black Stag. They turned up quite out of the blue, and Veronica and I are dining with them tonight."

"Such a delightful girl," said Mrs Vansittart. "Not a bit like the mannerless teenagers we seem to get around here. I suppose blood will tell, whatever the circumstances. Forgive me, my dear." She looked to make sure the housekeeper had duly closed the door behind her. "I'm glad to have a chance to tell you how wonderfully well I think you are behaving."

"Why, thank you," said Patience, amazed, and fled.

She found Veronica assembling bottles and glasses in the upstairs sitting room, already immaculate in long shirt and new jeans. "Will I do for the Black Stag?" she asked. "Wear your new trousers, Patience, please, to back me up!"

"As if you needed it." But time was short and it was the quickest possible change. Once again she admired the effect of the long red shirt, slung some black beads round her neck and went down to find Veronica rooting for crisps in the kitchen cupboard.

"Cool," she approved. "Golly, here they are!"

Mary was in a long ethnic shirt over trousers, and Mark had put on a tie inside his casual jacket. "How nice you all look," he said. "This is the best I can do. You'll have to stand by me if the Black Stag turns up its nose. I wasn't expecting formal dinners when I started out to meet Mary." He handed a bottle of champagne to Veronica. "I told them to chill it, but you might put it in the deep freeze for a minute while you find us some glasses."

"Cool," she said again. "I can cope, Patience, you go on up."

"What a nice child." Mary settled on the small sofa with the view across the garden to tree tops.

"Isn't she?" said Patience. "I'm so lucky." Mark seemed to have stayed downstairs with Veronica. And why not? "How did Mark get on with his telephoning?" She joined Mary on the sofa.

"Pretty well. He had a longer chat than he had intended with Grisel, who had been to more meetings about good causes in the last few days than you and I have in our lifetimes."

"Speak for yourself." Patience laughed. "My life was one long round of them when I was married to Geoffrey. Grisel's out of the running then?"

"Yes. And she said she hadn't heard from Ludwig and Leonora for donkey's years. Which means nothing either way. They never were a loving family."

"What about Seward?"

"She'd been to see him just yesterday. He's in a home in Wimbledon. She made it sound pretty horrible, Mark said. Everybody's nightmare. But he certainly wasn't loose down here trying to kill you."

"Which leaves Priss."

"Yes. And she was not answering her phone. The British Telecom lady took a message: Mark left this number. Better than the Black Stag. Then he tried Paul's office: he'd just left, the girl said. But he's been there seeing clients for the last few days. Mark managed to find that out casually. He left this number for him too."

"Number? For whom?" Mark appeared with a tray of champagne flutes, followed by Veronica with the bottle in its silver chilling jacket.

"Paul Protheroe," Mary told him. "I was telling Patience how you'd been getting on."

"Protheroe!" Veronica put down the bottle dangerously near the edge of the table. "But he's the one—"

"Which one?" Mark rescued the bottle and began to loosen the foil.

"The one who handled Mum's money! Who phoned me to say it stopped with her death. I didn't know anything about it, see. Not till he phoned. It just came into the bank. And then, after she died, it didn't. And, like, I did go and ask; it seemed pitiful not to, but they just said they didn't know. It had come. It had stopped. End of story. Then there was this phone call, and a girl said, 'I've Mr Protheroe for you'. And he came on and told me, oh so kindly, that the money stopped with Mum's death. It was an annuity, he said, so of course it did. He treated me as if I was some kind of young fool. Well, I suppose I was.

195

And, after, I couldn't remember. The name, I mean. It was all such a shock; happened so fast. And then all Mum's papers went on to the tip, so I couldn't check up on anything. That's when I went round the bend a bit."

"No wonder," said Mark. "But you're sure now that it was Protheroe?"

"Dead sure. All I could think of was Fothergill. Well, that would figure, wouldn't it?"

"It certainly would," said Mark. And then: "Patience, that's told you something, hasn't it?"

"I'll say it has. I can't believe it! But of course I do. You remember, Paul Protheroe was my trustee. That's when it all started. He took me out to lunch for my twenty-first and told me the money was all gone, used up on my education. My father had miscalculated, he said. Geoffrey and I always thought he had managed to embezzle it somehow, but Geoffrey said it wasn't worth going after him about it. It would only be money into lawyers' pockets, he said, so hard to prove fraud, and we had plenty from old Mrs Ffeathers. Just more misery for me, he said it would be. All the time he must have been using what he knew to blackmail Paul Protheroe. So when he needed to he could make him handle the funds for Veronica's mother. And then, when the two of them died, it must have been the same thing all over again. Paul didn't see why he should go on paying out good money to a girl who knew nothing about him. I suppose that must have been part of the arrangement with your mother, Veronica. That she wouldn't tell you anything about where the money came from."

"I never asked," said Veronica. "Why would I? I just grew up with it like that. And then, all of a sudden, she was dead.

There was so little time, and the ward full of people, listening. She talked about Father, a bit, but not about money. I just held her hand, mostly." She emptied her glass. "Well, she was busy dying."

"At least you were there, holding her hand," said Patience, and there was a little silence.

Mark broke it. "So, it's the Protheroes," he said.

"Priss," agreed Patience. "When Mrs Vansittart told us about the dark woman hanging around something tweaked in my mind. Do you remember that odd thing that happened to me years ago, before I ever came down to the Hall?" Again she spoke across Mary to Mark. "Being framed for shoplifting? That was a young woman with dark hair. And that was something else Geoffrey was happy to drop."

"Priss was fair," said Mary.

"I expect she used a wig." Mark shared out the last drops from the bottle. "But why would they have wanted to stop you coming to the Hall, Patience? Back then."

"They must have had some plan of their own. There's no way your Uncle Joseph would have told either his wife or his daughter what he and the others were planning. Priss must have thought me a threat to her inheritance from the old lady. I do remember, Paul Protheroe went off in a great hurry after lunch that day when he told me I was broke. He must have had a date with her to set it up, if I agreed to go down to the Hall. He knew I wasn't going to fetch the cape until just before my train left, so there would have been time. But I think she picked up the pearls to frame me with the day before. I remember the salesgirl was a bit puzzled about them. It really seemed a clear case," she explained to Veronica. "The pearls were in the pocket of a fur cape I was picking up for

197

Josephine Brigance, and this mysterious dark lady had told a
salesgirl she had seen me steal them. Only luckily for me I'd
met Geoffrey on the way in and he could vouch for me."

"Always Geoffrey," said Veronica, and Patience thought:
My God, he's her father.

There was another silence, broken this time by Mary. "Priss
was the only one who kept in touch with people down here,"
she said thoughtfully. "I suppose she must have been down
staying with her friends the Thompsons in Brighton. You did
say you went shopping there, Patience? The two of you?"

"Yes. That's right. She could have seen us, drawn her own
conclusions, and panicked."

"But how would she have known you were vulnerable like
that, through the area?"

"Oh, that's easy. She was always nosy, Priss. Everyone
knew I was buying this house, but of course it took a
while before it was all settled. She could have posed as a
prospective buyer and had a good look round. Maybe they
were planning something anyway." It was not a pleasant
thought. "Actually, I remember the estate agent threatening
me with a rival purchaser, but I just thought it was the usual
form of pressure. One good thing your telephone calls will
have done, Mark, bless you, will be to have warned her off,
don't you think? Now she and Paul know you two are here
as witnesses and back-up?"

"Glad to be useful," said Mark. "Worth burning up the
roads, wasn't it, Mary? And now, it's high time we went
and ate our dinner or the Black Stag will refuse us admission.
Let's talk strictly about cabbages and kings, shall we? Too
public there. Tomorrow will be time enough to think about
the next stage."

"But I thought—" began Mary.

"Such a mistake." He sounded for the first time like the frivolous young man Patience remembered. "Thinking time tomorrow." But as he helped Patience into her jacket she noticed him eyeing the tiny letter box she had meant to have replaced by a more postman-friendly one.

She caught his eye. "Only a very small letter bomb," she agreed. "But we'll tape it up before we go to bed, just for luck."

Eleven

That was a cheerful evening, with conversation seeming to flow spontaneously round the table, though Patience, on the alert for all kinds of reasons, noticed just how neatly Mark managed to give it a little shove forward when it was needed, and how careful he was to see that Veronica was not left out of things. But she was a young person very well able to hold her own, cheerfully ready with an opinion when she had grounds for one, but equally happy to listen or even to admit ignorance if necessary.

Mark seemed to have been all over the world, and Mary had gone out to meet him whenever she could. "Between marriages," she summed up her position lightly enough.

"You make me feel a terrible stay-at-home," Patience confessed over coffee. "Madeira at Christmas was quite far enough for Geoffrey." She met Veronica's eyes with a little pang of discomfort, wondering what she and her mother had done.

"You'll have to start travelling now." Mark was firmly signing the bill. "Nothing in the world to stop you."

"You're right. Shall we go somewhere really frivolous for Christmas, Veronica?" Why did the idea suddenly seem so depressing?

Mary was looking at her watch. "I hate to be a wet blanket, but I have to start back to town at the crack of dawn for an appointment. I don't like to leave you, Patience, but if Mark is staying for a bit you'll be OK. It's a consultant," she explained. "I've waited long enough for the appointment; mustn't miss it now. I'm sure it's a false alarm, but better safe than sorry."

"Oh, Mary." Patience reached out to clasp Mary's hand for a long, close minute. "I wish you'd told me." Impossible to ask for details now.

"I did mean to." They both remembered the fright Veronica's paint had given them. "But I'm almost sure it's all imagination really. It so often is."

"I do hope so. Promise to let me know what he says."

"Of course. I'll want to hear about you, too. Myself, I still think you ought to go to the police."

"That's what I say," said Veronica.

"Patience and I are going to talk it over in the morning," Mark told her.

"Not the morning," said Patience. "I've fixed to go and see my solicitor."

"Are you going to tell him?"

"Goodness, no. But I'm making a new will."

"Cutting us all out," he said with satisfaction. "Good. The afternoon then. Let's walk up the hill, if it's half-way decent weather. I haven't seen that view of yours for over forty years."

"And I'm going into Brighton," said Veronica. "To see a man Mark knows, about my A levels. He thinks he might sneak me in."

"Oh, bless you, Mark," said Patience and watched with an

odd little tweak of the heart as Mark tucked Veronica into her jacket.

Mark checked the area when he saw them home, and they taped up the letter box once they were inside, agreeing that they felt quite silly doing so. But Patience had a restless night just the same, waking from time to time out of an anxious dream she just could not remember.

The telephone rang while they were at breakfast, and Veronica, nearer, picked it up. She said, "Mark," on a rising note, and then: "Cool," and, "Yes, I'll tell her . . . That was Mark." She smiled across the table. "He's coming into Brighton this morning, said he thought he'd drop in on those Thompsons and find out, casual-like, if Priss really was staying with them. He'll ring when he gets back, he said to tell you. And if I'm going to meet him at the station I must dash. Sorry to leave you with the dishes."

"They're nothing." But the house felt very empty after she had left.

Mr Jones did nothing to cheer her up. He was appalled at the little she told him about Veronica. The mere fact of her existence shocked him quite enough, and Patience was glad indeed that she had decided to tell him nothing about how they had met. She had no intention of telling him about the attempt on her life either, which made it hard to explain her sense of urgency about the new will, though he brightened up at her mention of Mary and Mark. "The best of the lot," he said. "I'm glad to hear you are back in touch with them. But it's a sad business, Mrs Crankshaw, a sad, sad business. And, if I may ask, what are you going to say locally to explain Miss Lavolle if she is really going to stay with you?"

"We talked it over, she and I, and she felt very strongly that

only the truth would do. And I respect her for it, Mr Jones. So
we told Mrs Vansittart, the other night. To tell you the truth,
I was a little surprised that you were surprised today."

"Well, as a matter of fact Mrs Jones did say something last
night. I am afraid I told her it was totally impossible."

"You owe her an apology, Mr Jones."

"I really believe I do. If I had not heard it from your own
lips, Mrs Crankshaw . . . You are totally convinced?"

"Totally. And when you see Miss Lavolle, so will you be.
The likeness to Geoffrey is remarkable. She is in Brighton
today, trying to fix up to take her A levels next year. She
missed them this summer because she was nursing her
mother. I'm afraid she has had a very hard time of it, and
I feel I owe her everything I can do for her."

"But not so fast," he pleaded. "Take time to think it over,
Mrs Crankshaw, to get to know the girl. You know nothing
about her after all."

"Oh." Patience could not resist it. "Did Mrs Jones not hear
about her grandfather?"

"Her grandfather?"

"Lavolle," said Patience.

"Not the Duke?"

"Yes, the Duke." She saw with satisfaction that, probably
for the first time in her life, Veronica's grandfather had been
useful to her. Mr Jones might not be convinced, but at least he
was working towards the belief that there must be something
to be said for Veronica, however illegitimate. He agreed
reluctantly to set about drafting the new will, and to put
her holograph in his safe for the time being.

On her way home she paused at the bank to discuss an
account for Veronica, then dropped in to Leyning's thriving

203

delicatessen and bought the makings of a cold lunch in case Mark or Veronica, or both of them, should return in time.

She waited in vain and was finally making herself a sandwich when the phone rang. Mark at last. But he was speaking from London, he told her.

"I'm so sorry. My masters got me on my mobile and summoned me to an urgent meeting. I'm at Victoria, on my way to it. I'll call you when I get back. Tonight, I do hope. No walk today, alas. Forgive me, Patience? And be careful, you and Veronica. Please."

Patience threw the sandwich into the bin and made herself a cup of coffee. She had just settled, elbows on table, to drink it, when the door bell rang. Idiotic to tell her to be careful. But it was probably Mrs Vansittart, or the milkman, or the erratic post.

She recognised Priss at once, though she had changed enormously from the plain, downtrodden daughter at home. The mousy hair had auburn highlights now, and a very expensive cut, and the charcoal grey suit had come straight off the catwalk. As Patience hesitated, remembering Mark's warning, Priss spoke.

"Patience! I've got to talk to you. Please? Mark Brigance came to the Thompsons' today, asking if I was there. I was out, thank God, but I knew what it meant. I've been God's own fool, Patience. May I come in?"

"Priss." Patience stood for a long minute looking at her, wondering what to do. Across the road something caught her eye; a window curtain stirring ever so slightly. God bless Mrs Vansittart, she thought, and opened the door wider. "Yes, do come in. My neighbour across the road is wondering who I've got calling on me now. We keep a friendly eye on each other, here in Leyning." Closing the door behind Priss she thought for a moment that she had been mad to let her in. "I've just made some coffee. Come and join me."

"Thanks." She dropped her jacket on a chair, revealing a toning silk shirt. Lots of money there, well spent. "I've come to confess." Her eyes met Patience's for the first time. "Throw myself on your mercy, Patience. I've been such a fool. I tried to kill you. I was off my head with fright. I saw you in Brighton with Veronica Lavolle. I couldn't believe my eyes."

"How come you knew her?" Patience had been wondering about this.

"Paul and I had a holiday in St Ives a few years ago. At least, I thought it was a holiday. He said he wanted to do a gallery crawl, buy some pictures. As an investment, of course. He never does anything except for money. And then I began to wonder. He kept looking at pictures of this stunning model called Jennifer Lavolle. He didn't want to meet her, just look at pictures of her, and her daughter. I began to think there had to be something kinky about it. Well, he never married me for my looks. I got frightened, and angry, a bit. We've been a good team; I really thought it was going to break up. In the end, I blew it, went for him – and he roared with laughter and told me all about it. He just wanted to see how like your precious husband the daughter was. He thought it might come in useful one day, for another of his plans. We saw them in the end across the room at a private view and you could see the likeness even from there. But how in the world did you find out about her, Patience? It must have been a shock."

"Yes, it was." She was not going to discuss Veronica with Priss. "I'm adopting Veronica. I've changed my will in her favour."

"Damned unfair," said Priss bitterly. "You've no more right to the old woman's money than the man in the moon. I wish to God I'd managed to stop you in the first place, that day at Gogarty's."

"So it was you?"

"Of course. We were afraid you'd foul up what we were planning. And how right we were. Didn't think I had it in me, did you? Any of you! The thing I really minded about the old bitch dying like that was she never got to know how we had been fooling her, Paul and I. I was looking forward to telling her. Only, just sometimes, now, I wish none of it had happened. He frightens me sometimes, Paul. If he was to find out what a mess I've made of it down here I don't know what he'd do. And I love him, see, can't help it. Always have, always will. I did it for him. Tried to do it. But it didn't work. I kept listening to the news. Nothing!"

"I suppose it would have been all right if you had succeeded," said Patience dryly. "Managed to kill us both."

"Well, of course. That would have changed everything, wouldn't it? Both of you gone! A good honest accident with the gas, like there have been so many. Poor people with careless landlords." She sounded almost reproachful. "And now you say you have changed your will. Cut us all out."

"You knew you were in?"

"Oh, yes. I told you Paul's a clever fellow. He managed to infiltrate Mr Jones's office. That's what he called it and I don't ask questions. The less I know the better, he says, and I agree with him. Wouldn't you? I wish, now, I hadn't found out about the Lavolles. But it was only fair that we should inherit Gran's money in the end. You know perfectly well that was what she intended."

"And that entitles you to kill for it?"

"Paul was always sure you would leave it back to us. It was our old age insurance. He told me to come and take a look at this house when you bought it this summer, just in case. And then I saw you and the Lavolle girl in Marks and Sparks. Paul always said that if you two got together we were finished. Only there was no way you would. He'd made sure you knew nothing about her. As sure as you can be of anything. Why in the world would she get in touch with you, of all people?"

"You may well ask," said Patience; but that was all she said.

"Where is she now?"

"In Brighton again. Fixing up about her A levels, I hope. And Mark Brigance is in London, back any minute, so I advise you not to try anything, Priss."

"Oh, I'm beyond that. Do I have to go down on my knees, Patience? To get you to forget it ever happened? Tell no one?"

"Mark and Mary know. And Veronica, of course."

"But they're family. They won't talk if you don't. It's not just Paul. Please, Patience! It's the children, you see."

"Children? Priss, I didn't know."

"Twins. They're only twenty, Patience. I had them at the last gasp, when I'd almost given up hope. Paul had, I think, but we went on going through the motions, damned expensive, and then, suddenly, it worked. They're the best thing that ever happened to me, and to Paul. He adores them. They talk each other's language, he and they – you know what I mean? Internet and all that. If anything happened to spoil it, put them against him, I just don't know what he'd do. He might go right round the bend. Specially if he thought it was my fault. Patience, I'm begging you—"

The telephone rang. Patience picked it up. "Paul?" she said. And then: "Mark's not here, I'm afraid, but I can give him a message. I'm glad you called, actually. I've been wanting to talk to you. There are things we need to discuss, you and I. Could you lunch with me at the Black Stag, here in Leyning, tomorrow?" She listened: "Yes, I know it's short notice, but you see Veronica Lavolle is here, staying with me. I am going to adopt her. I'm sure you will see that this leaves a few things to be straightened out between you and me." And after another pause: "Good. Shall we say quarter to one in the front bar? I'll look forward to seeing you there."

She put the receiver down. It had given her time to think. "Don't worry," she told Priss. "I'm not going to say a word about you. You hadn't told Paul Veronica is here, had you?"

"I didn't dare. I told you, I'm afraid of him when he's angry. The twins aren't. I want it to stay that way. What are you going to say to him, Patience?"

"That's my affair. But nothing about you, and that's a promise. Now, tell me about the twins."

They were brilliant. "Quite beyond me," said their proud mother. "But Paul can keep up with them." They had chosen to go to different universities; the world was going to be their oyster.

Patience had made fresh coffee and Priss was on her third cup, still happily talking, when the front door bell rang.

"Patience!" Mark was on the doorstep. "You're all right? I got anxious about you." And then: "You've someone here?"

"Yes. Come in. It's Priss."

"So I was right."

"Well, yes and no." They were in the big kitchen now. "Priss, here's Mark."

"Oh!" Priss was already on her feet. "Mark! I'd not have known you." She picked up her jacket with shaking hands and he took it from her and eased her into it.

"Thank you. I must go. Patience, I can't . . . Please?"

"Don't worry, Priss. It's going to be all right, I think." She shepherded her out into the hall. "You're staying at the Thompsons', aren't you? Why don't you just stay on there until after I've seen Paul tomorrow? That way, bit of luck, this will be all sorted out and Paul won't be talking about it. You can go home and pretend you never saw Veronica and me."

"I wish to God I hadn't."

"Oh, no. Don't say that. I think it may end up all for the best really. It was time all this was cleared up, and now I think it's going to be. And no fret for the twins either."

"Oh, bless you, Patience! I'm so sorry." She turned back on the doorstep, tears in her eyes.

Patience nearly kissed her, changed her mind. "Don't fret; just forget all about it." She turned back into the house.

"Twins?" asked Mark.

"Brilliant twenty-year-old twins, a triumph of modern science, who must not know of their mother's little lapse from grace. She came to confess, Mark. When she heard you had called on the Thompsons, she knew the fat was in the fire. Poor creature, she's much more frightened of Paul's finding out about what she tried – and failed – to do than of anything we might do to her. And the twins mustn't know, of course. She painted a pretty dismal picture of their family life without realising it. I think she's a bit frightened of them, too. Imagine their finding out that their mother is a failed murderer . . . I'm afraid it was the failure she really regretted, but never mind that. And while she was begging me to keep her secret,

Paul rang, asking for you. So I invited him to lunch tomorrow at the Black Stag. You should have seen her face. But I'm not going to tell him. Not about her. I promised her."

"You look most enormously pleased with yourself." Mark picked a mug from the dresser. "Is there anything left in that pot? What are you planning for Paul?"

"Retribution." Patience filled the mug and passed him the biscuit tin. "When I was twenty-one Paul took me out to lunch and told me my money was all gone. Well, tomorrow I'm going to give him the best lunch the Black Stag can provide and set about a little genteel blackmail in return."

"Imitating your husband?"

"Just so. Oh, it is good to talk to someone who is so quick on the uptake!"

"It's mutual. So what are you going to threaten Paul with?"

"I suppose just what Geoffrey did. A full investigation of his finances. Priss said he told her once that if I ever met Veronica he was sunk. That's what panicked her into trying to kill us. Which has to mean that Geoffrey meant the fund he made Paul set up for Jennifer Lavolle to continue to her daughter, and Paul fudged it somehow so it reverted to him. He absolutely cannot afford to have me start an investigation. So I am going to sweetly suggest that he reconstitute the fund for Veronica and then I'll let bygones be bygones. After all, it's only fraud, Mark. No need to look so shocked."

"Not murder and a wicked attempt at a frame-up like my mama and her brothers tried against you, you mean? You're absolutely right, Patience. Fraud is the modern crime after all: perfectly respectable so long as you get away with it, and enough money is involved. And I do think you are right:

you'll have Protheroe in the hollow of your hand and be able to name your terms. I suppose you wouldn't let me join your happy little party?"

"I don't think it would work, do you? It has to be just the two of us."

"But there's nothing to stop me lurking in the background somewhere, eating my own lunch and keeping an eye in case he whips out the arsenic bottle and pours it over your salad."

"Goodness, yes, that would be a comfort. Not the arsenic, I mean. Your being there. But, Mark, don't you have to get back to work? From what Mary said I rather thought you must have overstayed your leave already."

"Quick, aren't you? I rather thought you'd noticed. And you are quite right as usual. Hence the summons today." He smiled at her across his mug and her heart gave something between a gasp and a hiccup. "Congratulate me. I'm a free man, Patience. I can't tell you how well I like it. I've been thinking about it for a while. The game's not what it used to be; the edges have got too blurred. We connive at each other's corruption, and anything goes so long as you can fix the media. I've seen good friends left to carry the can when they could have been saved by just a little courage. But that's not in plentiful supply up top. So when they started to carpet me, like a naughty boy who's overstayed his exeat, I just handed in my notice and left. I was sweating with fright about you, to tell you the truth. Crazy to leave you on your own here. No time to phone; I caught the train by a whisker and ran up across the graveyard, only to find you capably giving the enemy coffee."

"Not the enemy," said Patience. "Poor Priss. People are their own punishments really, aren't they? I didn't even make

211

her admit that it was she who tried to kill Geoffrey when
he was leaving the Hall all those years ago, but I suppose,
now, it must have been. And of course in a way I had to be
grateful to her for that, because it did take the heat off me
a bit, granted that I was snug in my cell at the time."

"Another of her 'accidents'," said Mark. "But why,
Patience?"

"Geoffrey must have asked a question that frightened her.
He was a good policeman."

"I'll take your word for it. No, that's not fair. I know he
was: I was scared rigid for my mama, that's why I behaved
like such an idiot. Patience—"

"But, Mark," she interrupted him, as what he had told her
gradually sank in. "Do you really mean you have lost your job
because of all this? Mary said it was your life; you loved it.
What are you going to do now?"

"It was my life," he said. "That's right. But now I have
got a better idea. I was rather thinking—" The phone rang.
"Damnation!"

Patience reached to answer it. "Oh, Veronica," she said.
"No, it's all right; Mark's here, eating all my biscuits. No, of
course, do. You've got your key, haven't you? No, I promise
not to wait up." She replaced the receiver and smiled at Mark.
"Veronica started worrying, too. She's run into a friend in
Brighton and they were thinking of going to the cinema
tonight, but she wanted to make sure I was all right first,
nice child."

"And you are?"

"And I am."

He reached across the table to take her hand. "Well, in
that case," he said, "I shall finish my sentence. I was rather

thinking, Patience, of asking you to marry me. We've wasted a lot of time, you and I. Need we waste any more? And don't say, 'Oh, Mark, this is so sudden', either. It's not sudden at all, and you know it. You should have said yes last time I asked you. You know you should. I sometimes wish I'd done a Lochinvar and carried you off. Or just into bed. But once I knew about my mother, it was hopeless. I was hopeless. Hence the cloak and dagger life. I won't say I've been celibate for your sake, Patience, but I've been faithful to you in my fashion. No serious commitments. *You* are my serious commitment. Always have been, always will. I was in Hong Kong last month when I finally learned of Crankshaw's death. I've been on my way back to you ever since."

"But we're old, Mark."

"Nonsense. And anyway, who wants to be old alone? We've probably got thirty years or so yet, you and I, the way things go these days. Let's make the most of them. As for old: come along upstairs, Patience, and I'll show you how old we are."

"But I haven't said yes."

"You don't need to. Every beautiful bit of you has been saying yes to me from the moment I walked in at your door yesterday. I like your house, Patience; I've one of my own in the south of France, by the way. Shall we go there for our honeymoon? And talking of honeymoons" – he was on her side of the table now, his arm round her waist – "come along, my love, and God bless that intelligent child, Veronica."

"I thought it was *her* . . ." They seemed to be going upstairs.

"That I wanted? You didn't! Oh, what a lovely fool."

"I wish I was younger."

213

"You don't need to be younger. You only need to be you."

"Oh, Mark!"

"Oh, Patience! But that's not the word! I've been patient long enough." Their first kiss set something on fire between them and then there was no more talking.

"I didn't know it could be like that," she said much later.

"I'm glad. It's not been for me either. You must believe that, Patience. Never, in all those lonely years."

"Oh, I do believe it." She stirred luxuriously against him. "Such a wasted, sad time, our past. Was I waiting for you always?"

"I like to think so. I used to think of you at the oddest times, Patience. When I was happy, I wasn't happy enough; and when I was afraid, which I often was, the worst of all was the thought of never seeing you again."

"Oh, Mark!"

"Oh, Patience." He was smiling down at her now and her limbs turned to water. "Would you think me a heartless monster if I said I was hungry? No lunch, come to think of it."

"Nor me, what with one thing and another." She sat up, leaning comfortably against him, as if she had done it all her life. "There's a steak in the deep freeze, I think, and a nice Australian red in the wine rack. Draw the curtains at the front of the house, would you, before you turn the light on? Mrs Vansittart is going to find all this quite exciting enough as it is."

"God bless her for watching over you. I suppose I could hardly expect a man's dressing gown in this house." He was pulling on trousers and shirt as he spoke. "Don't put on too many clothes, my love, this is only the intermission."

*　　*　　*

"It feels like Darby and Joan." She was grilling steak and onions while he tossed the salad.

"Yes, isn't it strange? We could have been doing this for ever."

But back in bed it did not feel like Darby and Joan at all. Much later, hearing a key in the lock, Patience said, "Goodness, there's Veronica."

"I like the way you say 'goodness'. May I borrow your dressing gown, love? I'll deal with Veronica." He opened the bedroom door and greeted her as she came tiptoeing up the stairs. "Congratulate me," he said. "Patience and I are engaged to be married."

"Well, I should hope so," said Veronica. "I'll make the breakfast, Patience," she said over his shoulder. "Sleep well, you two."

"What a nice child." Mark closed the door on her. "With all the right ideas."

Over breakfast, the two of them ganged up on Patience. "You can't let Paul Protheroe get away with it," insisted Veronica, "and go on and rip off other widows and orphans. This time you really have got to go to the police, Patience."

"Or at least to Mr Jones," Mark told her. "You have to tell him he's got a spy in his office. Let him decide what to do about it."

"But I promised Priss I wouldn't tell on her. It's not the police she's afraid of, it's Paul."

"Then maybe she'd be better off without him," Mark said. "There must be some way we can work out for you to alert Jones without involving Priss. Let him go to the police. Once they are on to all that fraud, they are bound to sort it, and

Protheroe should go down for a good long sentence. Time for his family to find how pleasant it is not to have him around."

"I keep thinking about the twins," Patience said. "And their brilliant careers. Look, why don't we wait and see what Paul says at lunch?"

"Very well," Mark stood up. "But I'm joining you for lunch, Patience. Everything is different today, thank God. You're not on your own any more."

"Why, nor am I." She looked from one to the other. "I've got a whole family. How lucky I am. Ring the Black Stag for me, would you, Veronica, and change my booking from two to three."

"Right." She reached for the telephone. "Oh," she said presently. "Thank you. I'll tell her." And, replacing the receiver: "A message for you, Patience. Mr Protheroe to say he can't meet you."

"Is that so?" Mark did not sound entirely surprised. "Pass me the phone, would you, Veronica. What's Protheroe's office number, Patience?" He dialled it. "I bet he's done a runner."

"I should have thought of that. Goodness, I wonder if he's taken Priss."

They were silent as Mark conversed briefly with what sounded like a flustered female voice. "Yes." He hung up. "Chaos in the office, and the staff in tears. You'd better ring Priss at the Thompsons', Patience, and break the news, if necessary. She may need time to consider her position."

"She may indeed. I don't know what to wish for her." She paused, phone in hand. "No, she'll be there. I was wondering why Paul bothered to leave the message for me. He knew I'd break it to her, the coward; didn't want to tell her himself."

She was proved right. Priss had heard nothing and dissolved into hysterical tears at the news, gently broken to her by Patience. "Do nothing. Say nothing," Patience advised her. "Stay where you are and let the Thompsons look after you. No, of course I won't tell." She rang off. "So that's that," she said. "It will unravel by itself now, don't you think, without any intervention from us. Poor Priss; poor twins."

"Better without him," said Veronica. "And talking of that, how soon do you want me to move out, Patience?"

"Nonsense," said Mark, before Patience could speak. "You're our family, Veronica. Besides, who's going to mind the house for us while we are on honeymoon?"

"Just so." Patience smiled at them both. "I was thinking in the night that we might make a flat for you in the attic, Veronica."

"Were you so?" asked Mark. And then, as she blushed helplessly: "The really important question, Patience, is what kind of a wedding you want. I hope you were thinking about that too."

"Well, I was actually. And I know just what I want. A nice old-fashioned church wedding here in Leyning. As quiet as we can make it."

"Which won't be very," Mark told her.

"May I look after your trousseau?" asked Veronica.

"And Mrs Vansittart in the front row, of course," said Mark.

Right on cue, the front door bell rang.